# A Clockwork Orange

Anthony Burgess was born in Manchester in 1917 and studied English at the university there. He was drafted into the army upon graduation in 1940 and spent six years in the Education Corps. After demobilization, he worked first as a college lecturer in speech and drama and then as a grammar-school master. From 1954 to 1960 he was an education officer in the Colonial Service, stationed in Malaya and Borneo, and it was while he was there that he started writing *The Malayan Trilogy* (published in Penguin as *The Long Day Wanes*). In 1959 Burgess was diagnosed as having an inoperable brain tumour and was given less than a year to live. He then became a full-time writer and, proving the doctors wrong, went on to write at least one book a year and hundreds of book reviews right up until his death in 1993.

A late starter in the art of fiction, Anthony Burgess had previously spent much creative energy on music, and in his lifetime he composed many full-scale works for orchestra and other media. His Third Symphony was performed in the USA in 1975 and *Blooms of Dublin*, his musical version of Joyce's *Ulysses*, was presented in 1982. He believed that with the fusion of the musical and literary forms lay a possible future for the novel. His many other works include *Inside Mr Enderby*, *Enderby Outside*, *The Clockwork Testament*, *Enderby's Dark Lady*, *Tremor of Intent*; *Honey for the Bears*; *Urgent Copy*; *Nothing Like the Sun*; *Man of Nazareth*, the basis of his successful TV script *Jesus of Nazareth*; *Earthly Powers*, which was voted the best foreign novel of 1980 in France; *The End of the World News*; *The Kingdom of the Wicked*, winner of the Prix Europa in Geneva; *The Piano Players*; *Any Old Iron*; *A Mouthful of Air*; *Home to QWERTYUIOP*, an anthology of his reviews and journalism; and two volumes of autobiography: *Little Wilson and Big God*, which was awarded the J. R. Ackerley Prize for 1988, and *You've Had Your Time*. *A Clockwork Orange* was made into a film classic by Stanley Kubrick and was dramatized by the RSC in 1990. His last novel, published in the spring of 1993, was *A Dead Man in Deptford*, based around the murder of Christopher Marlowe.

Anthony Burgess died in November 1993, and is survived by his second wife and his son. *The Times* described him as 'one of the cleverest and most original writers of his generation', and among the many people who paid tribute to him were David Lodge, who considered him 'an inspiration and example to other writers', and John Updike, who believed that 'The literary world seems much more sparsely populated with Anthony Burgess gone. He had the energy and the wide-ranging interests of a dozen writers ... [and] seemed not only a prodigious intellect, but an affectionate spirit, whose mind, like Ariel's, circled the globe in a few seconds.'

Blake Morrison was born in Skipton, Yorkshire. He is the author of two collections of poems, *Dark Glasses* and *The Ballad of the Yorkshire Ripper*; two critical studies, *The Movement: English Poetry and Fiction of the 1950s* and *Seamus Heaney*; a children's book, *The Yellow House*; a play, *The Cracked Pot*, adapted from Heinrich von Kleist's *Der Zerbrochene Krug*; the memoir *And When Did You Last See Your Father?* (1993), which won the Esquire/Waterstone's Prize for non-fiction and the J. R. Ackerley Award for autobiography; and *As If* (1997), a study of the James Bulger case. He co-edited, with Andrew Motion, *The Penguin Book of Contemporary British Poetry*, and a selection of his own poems appears in *Penguin Modern Poets: Volume I* (1995). Formerly literary editor of the *Observer* and the *Independent on Sunday*, he lives in London.

# ANTHONY BURGESS

# A Clockwork Orange

*With an Introduction by Blake Morrison*

PENGUIN CLASSICS

Published by the Penguin Group
Penguin Books Ltd, 80 Strand, London WC2R ORL, England
Penguin Group (USA) Inc., 375 Hudson Street, New York, New York 10014, USA
Penguin Group (Canada), 90 Eglinton Avenue East, Suite 700, Toronto, Ontario, Canada M4P 2Y3
(a division of Pearson Penguin Canada Inc.)
Penguin Ireland, 25 St Stephen's Green, Dublin 2, Ireland (a division of Penguin Books Ltd)
Penguin Group (Australia), 250 Camberwell Road, Camberwell, Victoria 3124, Australia
(a division of Pearson Australia Group Pty Ltd)
Penguin Books India Pvt Ltd, 11 Community Centre, Panchsheel Park, New Delhi – 110 017, India
Penguin Group (NZ), 67 Apollo Drive, Rosedale, North Shore 0632, New Zealand
(a division of Pearson New Zealand Ltd)
Penguin Books (South Africa) (Pty) Ltd, 24 Sturdee Avenue,
Rosebank, Johannesburg 2196, South Africa

Penguin Books Ltd, Registered Offices: 80 Strand, London WC2R ORL, England

www.penguin.com

First published by William Heinemann Ltd 1962
Published in Penguin Books 1972
Reprinted with an Introduction 1996
Reprinted in Penguin Classics 2000
044

Copyright © Anthony Burgess, 1962
Introduction copyright © Blake Morrison, 1996
All rights reserved

The moral right of the author of the Introduction has been asserted

Set in 10/12.5 pt Monotype Minion
Typeset by Rowland Phototypesetting Ltd, Bury St Edmunds, Suffolk
Printed in England by Clays Ltd, St Ives plc

978-0-141-18260-5

www.greenpenguin.co.uk

MIX
Paper from
responsible sources
FSC
www.fsc.org    FSC™ C018179

Penguin Books is committed to a sustainable
future for our business, our readers and our planet.
This book is made from Forest Stewardship
Council™ certified paper.

# Contents

# Introduction

It was the source of some unhappiness to Anthony Burgess that, of the fifty or more works which he published during his lifetime, *A Clockwork Orange* should be the most famous. He had, he believed, written better books and feared he would be remembered 'as the fountain and origin of a great film' – that is, as the man who wrote the novel from which Stanley Kubrick made the more celebrated movie. Why, he wondered, could the reading public not attend to his other achievements: the Enderby novels; the playful fictional explorations of Shakespeare; the critical guides to Joyce; the music, the libretti, the plays, even the journalism and reviews? He compared himself to Rachmaninoff, whose Prelude in C Sharp Minor, written as a boy, is better known than the works of his maturity. The letters Burgess received from students working on *A Clockwork Orange*, evidence though they were of the esteem in which he was held in Academe, did not console him. Irritated, even embittered, he pushed on with other novels, one of which, *Earthly Powers* (1980), won huge acclaim and contains what has become his most quoted sentence: 'It was the afternoon of my eighty-first birthday, and I was in bed with my catamite when Ali announced that the archbishop had come to see me.' But it is *A Clockwork Orange*, published in 1962 near the beginning of his career, which readers first associate with the name Anthony Burgess.

There are good reasons for this, nothing to do with Kubrick's film. Burgess was a prolific novelist but also a wayward one, brilliant at particulars, careless with the whole (he once said that he revised page by page, but that 're-writing a whole book would bore me'). In *A Clockwork Orange*, which is more like a novella than a novel, his powers were fully concentrated. There is the title, to begin with, a memorable and richly suggestive one adapted from a piece of slang: 'as queer as a clockwork orange' is a Cockney expression meaning very queer indeed (the meaning can be, but isn't necessarily, sexual), and Burgess could see its potential even before he had a story to go with it. There is the fearful symmetry of the book's tripartite structure. There is the dark enticingness of the hero, Alex. There is the vision of a near-future society, as frighteningly persuasive, however small the canvas, as the dystopias of George Orwell or Aldous Huxley: a youth culture in revolt, a corrupt police force, a government unable to govern. There is the devastatingly simple, yet profound, moral dilemma, which underlies the book: is it better for a man to choose to be bad than to be conditioned to be good? To which Burgess, not hedging his bets, answers clearly: yes.

Above all, there is the language of *A Clockwork Orange*, which is every bit as queer as the title might imply – Joyceanly queer in places, more demanding of the reader than most fiction, but exuberant in its inventiveness. Though other novelists, from Joyce to Russell Hoban, have also coined strange tongues, there is nothing in English quite like Burgess's novel, and no one who perseveres beyond the opening paragraphs is likely to forget the experience, difficult and disorienting though it can be. The disturbance isn't only in the language, but in the incidents which Alex, the narrator, uses language to relate:

'All right, Dim,' I said. 'Now for the other veshch, Bog help us all.' So he did the strong-man on the devotchka, who was still creech creech creeching away in very horrorshow four-in-a-bar, locking her rookers from the back, while I ripped away at this and that and the other, the others going haw haw haw still, and real good horrorshow groodies they were that then exhibited their pink glazzies, O my brothers, while I untrussed and got ready for the plunge. Plunging, I could slooshy cries of agony and this writer bleeding veck that Georgie and Pete held on to nearly got loose howling bezoomny with the filthiest of slovos that I already knew and others he was making up. Then after me it was right old Dim should have his turn, which he did in a beasty snorty howly sort of a way with his Peebee Shelley maskie taking no notice, while I held on to her. Then there was a changeover, Dim and me grabbing the slobbering writer veck who was past struggling really, only just coming out with slack sort of slovos like he was in the land in a milk-plus bar, and Pete and Georgie had theirs. Then there was like quiet and we were full of like hate, so smashed what was left to be smashed – typewriter, lamp, chairs – and Dim, it was typical of old Dim, watered the fire out and was going to dung on the carpet, there being plenty of paper, but I said no. 'Out out out out,' I howled. The writer veck and his zheena were not really there, bloody and torn and making noises. But they'd live.

'It was certainly no pleasure to me to describe acts of violence when writing the novel,' wrote Burgess in 1972, the year Stanley Kubrick's adaptation embroiled him in controversy over the film's, and book's, possible incitement to violence. Later, in his autobiography *You've Had Your Time*, less on the defensive, he put it more interestingly: 'I was sickened by my own excitement at setting it down.' Strictly speaking, the excitement here – the description of a gang rape – is Alex's, not Burgess's. But there is no denying that the book is most alive when its hero behaves wickedly, not when he is paying for his crimes. Like Milton, Burgess was of the Devil's party without knowing it. *A Clockwork Orange* was intended to be, and is, an affirmation of individual choice, including the choice to murder and rape. Its theology and ethics are impeccable. But to express them it uses, as Alex does, a cutthroat razor.

Much of the excitement in the passage above comes not from what Alex says, but how he says it: from his *slovos*. Burgess called this language *nadsat*, a transliteration of the Russian suffix for 'teen', and imagined that at the time and place the events in the novel occur (somewhere in Europe, circa 1972), it had become part of the culture, or sub-culture. The narrator's three *droogs* (from *drugi*, friends in violence), also speak *nadsat*, and, like him, have pleasingly rootless, Anglo-Russo-American names: Alex (*a-lex*: without, or outside, the law), Georgie, Pete and Dim. Their language is essentially Anglo-American (Russian readers would be more in need of a translation of the passage above than we are) but many of the words are Slavic in origin. *Groodies*, for example, comes from *grud* (breast), and *horrorshow* from *kharashó*, the neuter form of the Russian word for 'good', and thus a term of approbation (like the modern use of 'wicked'). *Yarbles*, meaning testicles, may owe something to the Russian word for apples, *yabloko* (Alex later greets a government official with 'Bolshy great yarblockos to thee and thine'). *Devotchka* is 'woman' or 'wife'. *Slovos* are words and *govoreeting* is the speaking of them. *Glazzies* are eyes, though here they are the pink eyes on the tip of *groodies*, and thus nipples. The body inspires some of Burgess's best inventions: *rookers* (from *ruka*) can be both arms and hands, and *nogas* both legs and feet (*sabogs* are worn on the latter); there is also the *litso* (face), *rot* (mouth), *zoobies* (teeth), *yahzick* (tongue), *guttiwuts* (stomach) and *gulliver* (head: a nod at Jonathan Swift). Other coinages are more obviously slangy. *Cancers* are cigarettes, *pretty polly* is rhyming slang for money (lolly), and to do something *oddy knocky* is to do it on your own. *Sinny* is the cinema, aptly enough, given the evil Alex is forced to consume there (and also given what the author himself would come to feel about Stanley Kubrick's film). Averse though Burgess was to lavatory humour, there is a touch of it in his word for God: *Bog*.

The old American edition of *A Clockwork Orange* carried a glossary of *nadsat* words. Burgess did not approve of this: in a novel which takes brainwashing as its subject, he intended his own form of brainwashing, which was to force readers to use a Russian dictionary. Though reading the novel requires some puzzle-solving, the meaning of a *nadsat* word is often clear from the context, or from Burgess's own glosses: a paragraph about the pleasures of *deng* obligingly ends: 'But as they say, money isn't everything.' One reviewer described the language as 'out-of-this-world gibberish', but there is nothing random or otherworldly about it: Burgess chose his 200 or so words of *nadsat* because they work in English, whether as poetry, or humour (what could be more comical than policemen being *millicents*?), or plausible slang. Being a devotee of *Finnegans Wake*, he believed the more layers of ambiguity, the better. Thus the word for 'work' is *rabbit*, which owes something to the Russian verb *rabotat*, but may also suggest *rab* (Russian for 'slave'), and carries an echo of 'robot', and in Alex's vocabulary suggests scaredy behaviour. But Russian imports aren't the only aspect of the language. There are also, in the above passage, the repetitions ('creech creech creeching away'), the echoes of Shake-speare (to my ear, 'untrussed' comes in this category), and the wonder-fully laconic use of the word 'like': 'Then there was like quiet and we were full of like hate.'

This use of 'like' was probably rare in 1962, but became common-place in the counter-culture of the late 60s, as did the hallucinogenic drugs (the milk-plus) which Alex uses for recreation. Much about *A Clockwork Orange* is prophetic: by keeping his ear to the ground, Burgess sometimes heard the rumble of what was coming next. Tele-vision, for example, in Britain at least, was in its infancy in 1962: no satellite stations, no Eurotrash, no sign of Rupert Murdoch's global village. But Alex describes 'what they called a worldcast, meaning that the same programme was being viddied by everybody in the world that wanted to, that being mostly the middle-aged middle-class lewd-ies. There would be some big famous stupid comic chelloveck or black singer, and it was all being bounced off the special telly satellites in outer space, my brothers'. But novels set in futures – from Jules Verne's to J. G. Ballard's – have to be judged as novels, not by the accuracy of their predictions. When Alex wakes and looks at his bedside clock – 'oh eight oh oh hours' – the pleasure lies more in the protesting language (Alex, like most teenagers, would rather be asleep at this hour) than in the prophecy that time would become, as it has, digital. At the start of *A Clockwork Orange* the dress of Alex and his droogs is quasi-Elizabethan: 'a pair of black very tight tights with the old jelly mould, as we called it, fitting on the crotch'. By the end, three years later, fashions have changed: 'very wide trousers and a very loose black shiny leather like jerkin over an open-necked shirt with a like scarf tucked in. At this time too it was the heighth of fashion to use the old britva on the gulliver, so that most of the gulliver was like bald and there was hair only on the sides. But it was always the same on the old nogas – real horrorshow bolshy big boots for kicking litsos in.' It doesn't matter that some of this looks familiar – skinhead, or even vaguely punk – and some of it much less so. Burgess's business was fiction, not futures. *A Clockwork Orange* also includes the ominous dreams which Alex and his father have the night before he loses his freedom – prophecies which belong more in the tradition of Shakespeare's history plays than of *Brave New World* or Arthur C. Clarke.

Dismissing these dreams, Alex slips into Shakespearian or Biblical English. 'O my father . . . Fear not. He canst taketh care of himself, verily.' He also slips into the third person, though this is unusual, and a joke. One of Burgess's triumphs is to let Alex tell his own tale, rather than keeping him at a safe distance. Alex insinuates and allies himself so intimately with his readers ('O my brothers') that we end up sharing every laugh ('haw haw haw') and cry ('boohoohoo'). He may not be as seductive a young narrator as Holden Caulfield in J. D. Salinger's *The Catcher in the Rye*, but he has the same undeceived attitude to adults, and all their phoney values. The work ethic has crushed his poor 'pee and em' (father and mother) to the point where he feels pitying contempt for them. Life is dull, made tolerable only by drugs, sex and violence. Bourgeois comforts hold no attraction: 'HOME,' Alex reflects, spotting the name on the gate of a country cottage, 'a gloomy sort of a name.' He is a classic teen anti-hero, and this includes him having a quality of innocence, even at his most depraved. Deceived by his droogs and arrested for murder, he is then conned by his fellow cons, who put sole blame on him for a second murder, that of a new inmate. Later, having naïvely consented to Reclamation Treatment (which succeeds in making him nauseous every time he contemplates violence), he becomes a pawn in a political struggle between government and opposition: the Augustinians in power, who use him as a guinea pig for their experiment in human conditioning; and the seemingly liberal but no less ruthless Pelagians, who want to parade him as a victim of government tyranny. (The distinction here was one Burgess often made himself: St Augustine thought that man is born in original sin, the monk Pelagius denied the doctrine.) Alex is too brutal to be wholly sympathetic and too strong to be a victim. But like many a rebel-hero, he exudes diabolic charm.

One of Alex's charms is his love of music, which he plays full blast in his typically teenage bedroom ('Here was my bed and my stereo, pride of my jeezny, and my discs in their cupboard, and banners and flags on the wall'), and which lifts him to lyric heights: 'Oh, it was gorgeousness and gorgeosity made flesh. The trombones crunched redgold under my bed, and behind my gulliver the trumpets three-wise silverflamed, and there by the door the timps rolling through my guts and out again crunched like candy thunder. Oh, it was wonder of wonders. And then, a bird of like rarest spun heavenmetal, or like silvery wine flowing in a spaceship, gravity all nonsense now, came the violin solo . . .' What distinguishes Alex from most teenagers is that his tastes in music are classical: Bach, Mozart, above all Beethoven, whose Ninth Symphony becomes the novel's dominant motif. It may reflect Burgess's own prejudices that, feeling some affection for his hero, he could not permit him to be a devotee of pop. There was also the consideration that a love of Elvis Presley or Billy Fury would have dated the novel. More than this, though, Burgess uses music to address the question of whether high art is civilizing. The fact that the men who ran Auschwitz read Shakespeare and Goethe, and played Bach and Beethoven, was much discussed at the time Burgess was writing *A Clockwork Orange*: the essays collected in George Steiner's *Language and Silence* (which Burgess reviewed on its publication in 1967) repeatedly address it. Alex addresses it too, laughingly dismissing the old Leavisite notion that art humanizes: 'I had to have a smeck, though, thinking of what I'd viddied once in one of these like articles on Modern Youth, about how Modern Youth would be better off if A Lively Appreciation Of The Arts could be like encouraged. Great Music, it said, and Great Poetry would like quieten Modern Youth down and make Modern Youth more Civilized. Civilized my syphilised yarbles. Music always sort of sharpened me up, O my brothers, and made me feel like old Bog himself, ready to make with the old donner and blitzen and have vecks and ptitsas creeching away in my ha ha power.' It's a black mark against the government psychologist Dr Brodsky that, himself uninterested in music, he uses Beethoven in his reform programme, so that Alex, thereafter, can never hear Beethoven play without feeling sick. The opposition liberals, too, wilfully torture Alex with the Ninth Symphony, driving him to attempt suicide. Music may not civilize Alex, but it is an essential mark of his good taste and of his enemies' lack of it.

The government's reform programme is called the Ludovico Method, a play on Beethoven's first name. *A Clockwork Orange* finds room for many literary jokes and allusions of this kind. The masks Alex and his gang wear to disguise themselves when committing crimes are those of Disraeli, Henry VIII, Elvis Presley and Peebee Shelley. A singer heard in the milk-bar stereo is Johnny Zhivago. There is a Kingsley Avenue and a Priestly Place, roads which allow Burgess to pay tribute to British contemporaries of his – as do Marghanita (Laski) Boulevard, (Angus) Wilsonsway, and (Bob) Boothby Avenue. Burgess even works himself into the story in the form of F. Alexander, the man whose wife is raped in the passage above. Alexander's name links him with Alex, whom he later meets again, by which time his wife has died, as a result, it seems, of the rape. He is also the author of a book called *A Clockwork Orange*. This book doesn't sound like Burgess's – it is, says Alex, 'written in a very bezoomny like style, full of Ah and Oh and that cal', and bears more resemblance to Colin Wilson's existentialist polemic *The Outsider* – but when Alexander speaks up for individual choice and freedom it is in words very like his author's. The effect here is of an endlessly receding mirror. There is another image in the mirror, too. In 1944, while Burgess was serving in Gibraltar, his first wife, Lynne, was beaten, kicked and robbed in London by a gang of four GI deserters. She suffered a miscarriage as a result, and Burgess once speculated, in an interview, that her poor health and early death may have had something to do with the attack. ('CLOCK-WORK ORANGE GANG KILLED MY WIFE – AUTHOR' ran the headline in the London *Evening News*.) The fictionalizing of this episode in *A Clockwork Orange* was a catharsis for Burgess, and, as he once said, 'an act of charity' to his wife's assailants, since he chooses to write it as if from their point of view rather than their victim's.

This is not the only element of autobiography underlying the book's composition. Burgess wrote the first draft in 1960 when, returning to Britain from Malaya and Brunei, where he had worked for six years as an education officer in the Colonial Service, he was diagnosed as suffering from an inoperable brain tumour and told (via his wife) that he had only a year to live. He was 43, with four novels behind him. Rather than embark on an exotic holiday or adventure, as condemned men are expected to do, Burgess settled down in Hove, on the south coast of England, with the intention of writing several novels before the year was out, thus providing his wife with a stream of posthumous royalties. Burgess had been an occasional novelist up to this point, writing fiction between teaching, composing music and other impecunious pursuits. Now, under a death-sentence, he became a professional:

The practice of a profession entails discipline, which for me meant the production of two thousand words of fair copy every day, weekends included. I discovered that, if I started early enough, I could complete the day's stint before the pubs opened. Or, if I could not, there was an elated period of the night after closing time, with neighbours banging on the walls to protest at the industrious clacking. Two thousand words a day means a yearly total of 730,000. Step up the rate and, without undue effort, you can reach a million. This ought to mean ten novels of 100,000 words each. The quantitative approach to writing is not, naturally, to be approved. And because of hang-overs, marital quarrels, creative deadness induced by the weather, shopping trips, summonses to meet state officials, and sheer torpid gloom, I was not able to achieve more than five and a half novels of very moderate size in that pseudoterminal year. Still, it was very nearly E. M. Forster's whole long life's output.

The five and a half novels which Burgess produced in his *annus mirabilis* were *The Doctor is Sick, Inside Mr Enderby, The Worm and the Ring* (a reworking of an earlier draft), *One Hand Clapping, The Eve of Saint Venus* (a novella which had begun as an opera libretto) and *A Clockwork Orange*. In its first, half-completed, version, which he put aside at the end of the year, realizing he might after all have time to return to it, *A Clockwork Orange* already had its theme and futuristic setting. Newly back in Britain, Burgess had been struck by the development of coffee bars, pop music and teenage gangs. In particular, there was the rivalry between Mods and Rockers, whose violent Bank Holiday clashes – in Brighton and Hastings – he was in a good position to observe. For his novel, Burgess posited a near future, the 1970s, in which adolescent violence had become large enough a social problem for the government to resort to Pavlovian techniques of 'negative reinforcement'. The difficulty he had on the first draft was with the novel's language. Always fascinated by slang, dialect, neologism, obscenity and the argot of sub-groups, Burgess was receptive to the new teenage vernacular. But he worried about its ephemerality: the danger in using the idiom of Mods and Rockers was that it would be outdated by the time the novel was published, let alone a generation later. Reluctantly, Burgess shoved the first draft in a drawer and got on with something else.

He went back to it the following year, 1961, when, by chance, he found a solution to his stylistic quandary. He and his wife had decided to take a holiday in Leningrad, and in preparation he set about re-learning Russian, which he had studied as a younger man. It occurred to him that, as he puts it, 'the vocabulary of my space-age hooligans could be a mixture of Russian and demotic English, seasoned with rhyming slang and the gipsy's bolo'. The Russo-Anglo-American patois which Burgess devised had the additional bonus, as far as he was concerned, of suggesting that male adolescent aggression was not merely a local British phenomenon. Indeed once Burgess reached the Soviet Union for his holiday, he saw that the Marxist authorities were having their share of problems with rebellious – though not politically dissident – teenage gangs. He even experienced the criminal under-world at first hand by indulging in a little black marketeering of his own, though not strictly in the spirit of research: hard-up as always, and needing to subsidize the holiday, he had filled two suitcases with polyester dresses from Marks and Spencer's in Tunbridge Wells, and sold these garments at a profit in the underground lavatories of his hotel. Perhaps this subterranean criminality fed an observation or two into the novel. But, in fact, the revision of A Clockwork Orange was almost complete before Burgess set sail for Leningrad from Tilbury.

The novel finally appeared in Britain in May 1962. With three more books having appeared in the meantime, Burgess now enjoyed a growing reputation, and had hopes that this novel might dramatically boost it – and also boost his income. These hopes were raised when he was interviewed, and the first chapter of A Clockwork Orange dramatized, on the BBC television programme Tonight, which in those days of only two channels was said to have an audience of nine million. But the novel, so Burgess claims in his autobiography, 'sold badly, rather worse if anything than previous novels of mine', a mere three thousand copies by the time his next royalty statement came through. The problem was over-exposure, he decided: the book had been so comprehensively discussed that readers felt they didn't need to go out and buy it. The reviews weren't encouraging, either. The consensus was typified by the *New Statesman*'s verdict that the novel was 'a great strain to read'. The *Times Literary Supplement* was harsher still: 'a nasty little shocker'.

In the US, where it came out later in the same year, *A Clockwork Orange* had a better reception. 'Burgess has written that rare thing in English letters – a philosophical novel,' said *Time*. But pleasure in the accolades was muted, since American reviewers were responding to a different version of the novel, minus the last chapter. Burgess's US publishers were W. W. Norton, whose vice-president, Eric Swenson, had been disinclined to publish the book unless the affirmative ending – in which Alex, on reaching maturity, renounces violence – was dropped. In Swenson's mind, this was not a condition of publishing but 'merely a suggestion made for conceptual reasons'. But whether gently invited or brusquely told to drop the ending, Burgess felt in no position to argue: he needed the advance, was pessimistic about finding an alternative US publisher, and knew his financial security rested on getting his name known on the other side of the Atlantic. The twenty-first chapter was therefore cut – and not restored in the US until 1988, twenty-six years later. In the preface he wrote to that 1988 edition, 'A Clockwork Orange Resucked', Burgess portrays himself as an Alex-like pawn, caught up in a political struggle that went way beyond commercial publishing: 'My book was Kennedyan and accepted the notion of moral progress. What was really wanted was a Nixonian book with no shred of optimism in it.'

Perhaps the first author ever, if his version of events is to be believed, to suffer from an American need for *pessimism*, Burgess had the comfort of knowing that foreign translations of the book, into French, Italian, Spanish, Catalan, Romanian, Russian, Hebrew and German, were based on the English version. Yet most people know *A Clockwork Orange* in its truncated US version. Why? Because this was the text which Stanley Kubrick worked from when he came to make his film of the novel in 1972. Burgess had known of Kubrick's project before he was invited by Warner Brothers to a private preview of the film, in London, in the autumn of 1971. He had even written a script, which, like several others, Kubrick had rejected. It seems surprising, in the circumstances, that Kubrick was not aware of the unabridged English version, but if Burgess's autobiography is to be trusted it was the author himself who apprised him of it after the private screening. It was the source of some tension between them – along with the fact that Burgess had sold the film rights for a pittance to Kubrick's producers, and reaped no benefit when it became a huge international success. There may have been some competitiveness, too, exacerbated by the implication of some critics that though Burgess was the originator of *A Clockwork Orange*, Kubrick was its true artistic spirit. An interviewer in the *Transatlantic Review*, James B. Hesemath, put this thought with embarrassing bluntness in 1976, suggesting to Burgess that he'd been a 'lesser English novelist', whose novel had been 'more or less forgotten', until Kubrick's film. Burgess was understandably touchy at the suggestion, and replied that, if anything, Kubrick was a creation of *his*.

There were other tensions. Burgess had been an admirer of *2001: A Space Odyssey*, and hoped the film of *A Clockwork Orange* would aspire to a similarly imaginative 'visual futurism'. He was to be disappointed. In the novel, the rapes, attacks and knifings of Alex and his gang are partly veiled by language: as the author explained, 'to *tolchock* a *chelloveck* in the *kishkas* does not sound as bad as booting a man in the guts.' Kubrick's film uses equivalent veiling or parodic techniques, but to Burgess the violence felt stark and unfiltered none the less. Privately, he was worried, and – a Catholic, after all, sensitive to these matters – suspected the film of being pornographic. Publicly, he did not feel able to denounce it, and when it was released in the US in December 1971 he was soon caught up in the publicity. Early in 1972 he wrote an enthusiastic article about the film from New York for *The Listener*, describing it as 'very much a Kubrick movie, technically brilliant, thoughtful, relevant, poetic, mind-opening'.

By this point, the film was becoming a *cause célèbre*, and with

Kubrick himself reluctant to defend his moral purpose, it was Burgess who appeared on chat shows (often in the company of the film's lead actor, Malcolm McDowell) to explain what *A Clockwork Orange* had intended. The attendant publicity had its farcical moments: in New York, an Indian (or native American) threatened him with a tomahawk, and a striptease artist, enclosing her photograph, offered to come to his bed. But there was a serious side to the controversy. The film, and book, were accused of being an incitement to violence. In Britain, questions were asked in Parliament, and the banning of the film was urged. In the US, it was reported that four boys, dressed in droog style, had gang-raped a nun in Poughkeepsie. The report was inaccurate (the boys had not seen the film), but the charges of immorality did not go away. In due course Kubrick himself withdrew the film from distribution in Britain, where it remains unavailable to this day. Burgess felt his novel's reputation had been permanently tainted.

Always resourceful, Burgess used some of these experiences in his novella *The Clockwork Testament*, written in ten days in 1974 and featuring his old alter ego Enderby, here the author of a screenplay based on Gerard Manley Hopkins's *The Wreck of the Deutschland* which becomes a controversial film. The scenes include an excruciating television interview, and convey something of Burgess's strange experiences on the chat-show circuit. If it fails as a novel, it may not only be because it was written too quickly, but because of Burgess's essential ambivalence towards Kubrick's film. In 1987, he produced his own dramatic version of *A Clockwork Orange*, 'a play with music', intended to provide a definitive text which would stem the flow of bad amateur stage versions, but also be a kind of reproach to Kubrick, showing him how the novel might be adapted visually without distorting its spirit. (A stage direction at the end of Act Two reads: 'A man bearded like Stanley Kubrick comes on playing, in exquisite counterpoint, *Singin' in the Rain* on a trumpet. He is kicked off the stage.') The crucial point about this play version is that it includes the book's final chapter.

The lopping of this chapter from Kubrick's film, and from the US edition of the novel, infuriated Burgess for two reasons. First, there is the violation of the book's structural – even numerological – unity. Burgess divides *A Clockwork Orange* into three sections, each beginning with the same punkily defiant question: 'What's it going to be then, eh?' There are twenty-one chapters in all: twenty-one is the age at which children traditionally become adult, and it is in the twenty-first chapter that Alex sees the light and puts the errors of youth behind him. Burgess would also have been struck by the aptness, in a novel about growing up, of there being seven chapters in each section: an implicit allusion to Shakespeare's seven ages of man. As all this suggests, *A Clockwork Orange* is the most carefully constructed of novels.

Burgess's second objection to the loss of the last chapter is that it destroys the book's moral integrity. He felt there was little point in writing a novel which didn't allow for moral growth, and found something glib, cynical and sensationalizing in the abridgement. Alex is often called 'amoral', and it's true that, to begin with, he lives for the present, having few hopes of the future. 'Why, you've got everything in front of you,' he's told, cheerily, to which he replies, bitterly: 'Yes . . . Like a pair of false groodies.' But his willingness to learn from those older than himself – or as he puts it, 'to slooshy what some of these starry decreps had to say about life and the world' – is established as early as Chapter 2. It is picked up again later, when, in prison, he reads the Bible for enlightenment and comfort (though after his cure, the Bible, like Beethoven, turns him off: 'all I found was about smiting seventy times seven and a lot of Jews cursing and tolchocking each other, and that made me want to be sick'). All this prepares the ground for Alex's reform. There is no *deus ex machina* in his eventual getting of wisdom. All he lacks is time, and the three years that pass in the course of the book are what make the difference. The final chapter opens with Alex in a milkbar with his three droogs and seemingly back to his old *tolchocking* ways. The first hint of change comes when he refuses to buy the usual round for the women at the bar: 'I don't like just throwing away my hard-earned pretty polly, that's what it is.' Alex tells his droogs he has 'some thinking to do', and accidentally reveals, to their derision, that he's in the habit of carrying a picture of a baby in his wallet. He has a new taste for romantic music, too, for *Lieder*, 'very quiet and like yearny'. 'It was like something soft getting into me,' he reflects as he walks the streets alone. Ripe for conversion, his epiphany comes when he meets his old friend Pete, and is introduced to his wife. Envying Pete, Alex dreams of family comforts he'd like for himself: the hot meal on the table, the warm fire, the companionship, the baby gurgling in the cot. The change is on him:

Yes, yes, yes, there it was. Youth must go, ah yes. But youth is only being in a way like it might be an animal. Not, it is not just like being an animal so much as being like one of these malenky toys you viddy being sold in the streets, like little chellovecks made out of tin and with a spring inside and then a winding handle on the outside and you wind it up grrr grrr grrr and off it itties, like walking, O my brothers. But it itties in a straight line and bangs straight into things bang bang and it cannot help what it is doing. Being young is like being like one of these malenky machines.

My son, my son. When I had my son I would explain all that to him when he was starry enough to like understand. But then I knew he would not understand or would not want to understand at all and would do all the veshches I had done, yes perhaps even killing some poor starry forella surrounded with mewing kots and koshkas, and I would not be able to really stop him. And nor would he be able to stop his own son, brothers. And so it would itty on to like the end of the world, round and round and round, like some bolshy gigantic like chelloveck, like old Bog Himself (by courtesy of Korova Milkbar) turning and turning and turning a vonny grahzny orange in his gigantic rookers.

But first of all, brothers, there was this veshch of finding some devotchka or other who would be a mother to his son. I would have to start on that tomorrow, I kept thinking. That was something like new to do. That was something I would have to get started on, a new like chapter beginning.

Eric Swenson, Stanley Kubrick and a number of critics have found this last chapter too blandly optimistic: to end with Alex's cynical return to his violent ways ('I was cured all right') is, they say, tougher and more realistic. But this is to ignore the continuing pessimism that qualifies Burgess's happy ending. Alex may reach maturity, but his son will later have to pass through adolescence and all the mayhem it entails – 'And so it would itty on to like the end of the world, round and round and round.' There is no callow triumphalism here. Alex will have his descendants, and Burgess sees no means of stopping the cycle of adolescent violence, except with methods, whether aversion therapy, eugenics or other forms of socio-psychological programming, which are dehumanizing, morally unacceptable and a usurpation of God.

This leaves the question of whether *A Clockwork Orange* is not, as Burgess self-accusingly put it, 'a work too didactic to be artistic', 'pure art dragged into the arena of morality'. Novelists, it's agreed, should show, not tell, but science fiction invariably has an urgent moral purpose, which makes it a suspect genre. Burgess himself wrote two other allegories, or futfics: *The Wanting Seed*, published in the same year as *A Clockwork Orange*, which imagines a world so overcrowded and short of food that cannibalism has become widespread; and *1985*, a response to Orwell's *Nineteen Eighty-Four*, a novel which had made a deep impression on him. 'Dystopias or cacotopias are only a kind of warning to hang on to what freedom one has,' Burgess once said, and the freedom he felt to be under threat when he wrote *A Clockwork Orange* was that of individual choice. His immediate target was the American psychologist B. F. Skinner, who believed that the work he had carried out on behaviour modification in animals could be brought to the human domain. An heir to Pavlov and the conditioned response, Skinner wanted to abolish notions of man as an autonomous, free agent, and had a vision of a planned society. His 'inventions' included teaching machines and mechanical baby-minders, and he also published a utopian novel, *Walden Two*, which imagines a society where 'We can achieve a sort of control under which the controlled, though they are following a code much more scrupulously than was ever the case under the old system, now *feel free*.' Behind Skinner lay other frightening theories of people-control, including the experiments of Nazi doctors. Burgess was also disturbed by accounts of new behaviourist methods of reforming criminals. His book, even before Kubrick's film, caught the anti-mechanistic spirit of the culture, or counter-culture, of the sixties, and took its place, somewhat awkwardly, alongside Ken Kesey's *One Flew Over the Cuckoo's Nest*, the works of R. D. Laing, and other books attacking the erosion of individual rights by penal and medical institutions.

There is certainly a danger, especially in its middle section, of *A Clockwork Orange* becoming a one-sided protest against mind-control. But even there Burgess doesn't silence argument, but makes it part of the novel's texture, as a debate unfolds between the prison 'charlie' or chaplain (who may owe something to Graham Greene's whisky priest), the government psychologist, Dr Brodsky, and the 'Minister of the Inferior':

'Choice,' rumbled a rich deep goloss. I viddied it belonged to the prison charlie. 'He has no real choice, has he? Self-interest, fear of physical pain, drove him to that grotesque act of self-abasement. Its insincerity was clearly to be seen. He ceases to be a wrongdoer. He ceases also to be a creature capable of moral choice.'

'These are subtleties,' like smiled Dr Brodsky. 'We are not concerned with motive, with the higher ethics. We are concerned only with cutting down crime —'

'And,' chipped in this bolshy well-dressed Minister, 'with relieving the ghastly congestion in our prisons.'

There's not much doubt whose voice Burgess sympathizes with here: in what he intended as an 'allegory of Christian free will', his support goes to the chaplain. Alex must be able to *choose* to be good; he must be an orange, capable of growth and sweetness, not a wound-up clockwork toy. But defending Alex's human rights is not the same as glamorizing his crimes. Another voice we hear is that of the old drunk set on by Alex and his droogs, who speaks for all the ordinary, innocent citizens who suffer at the hands of the brutal young: 'What sort of a world is it at all? Men on the moon and men spinning round the earth like it might be midges round a lamp, and there's not no attention paid to earthly law nor order no more.' Space may have been conquered, but life on earth is getting worse. The lodger whom Alex's parents take in during his imprisonment also rants against the selfish young and their mindless crime. But the government attempt to defeat criminals like Alex by depriving them of their minds – a literal form of mindlessness – is no solution. Youth, Burgess seems to be saying, must have its fling, however wild. A well-run state will moderate the dangers. But ultimately the only cure is age. In the preface to his play version of *A Clockwork Orange*, Burgess quotes *The Winter's Tale*: 'I would there were no age between ten and three-and-twenty, or that youth would sleep out the rest; for there is nothing in the between but getting wenches with child, wronging the ancientry, stealing, fighting.'

*A Clockwork Orange* went on nagging away at Burgess right up until his death in November 1993. In March that year, one month after the murder of a two-year-old child in Liverpool, James Bulger, by two ten-year-olds, Burgess reflected, in an article for the *Observer*, whether his novel might not have contributed in a small way to a 'cult of violence' among the young. 'There are beliefs we cling to and will not let go,' he wrote:

it must be considered a kind of grace in my old age to abandon a conviction that was part of my blood and bone. I mean the conviction that the arts were sacrosanct, and that included the sub-arts, that they could never be accused of exerting either a moral or an immoral influence, that they were incorrupt, incorruptive, incorruptible. I have quite recently changed my mind about that.

This protective attitude to the arts was really a desire to justify the corrupt elements in the greatest literature of all time. That of the Elizabethan stage. It was a wish not to see William Shakespeare as a violent writer . . .

But I begin to accept that, as a novelist, I belong to the ranks of the menacing.

There are echoes here of the late Yeats asking himself, 'Did that play of mine send out/Certain men the English shot?' But it is not quite the *mea culpa* it may seem: Burgess continues to defend A *Clockwork Orange* in the article, insisting that it taught, at most, 'a *style* of aggression', not aggression itself. Even so, he concedes too much. *A Clockwork Orange* needs no apology. It is a work of the highest artistic and moral integrity, as relevant now, and as linguistically alive, as it was when it first appeared.

# A Clockwork Orange

# Part One

## 1

'What's it going to be then, eh?'

There was me, that is Alex, and my three droogs, that is Pete, Georgie, and Dim, Dim being really dim, and we sat in the Korova Milkbar making up our rassoodocks what to do with the evening, a flip dark chill winter bastard though dry. The Korova Milkbar was a milk-plus mesto, and you may, O my brothers, have forgotten what these mestos were like, things changing so skorry these days and everybody very quick to forget, newspapers not being read much neither. Well, what they sold there was milk plus something else. They had no licence for selling liquor, but there was no law yet against prodding some of the new veshches which they used to put into the old moloko, so you could peet it with vellocet or synthemesc or drencrom or one or two other veshches which would give you a nice quiet horrorshow fifteen minutes admiring Bog And All His Holy Angels and Saints in your left shoe with lights bursting all over your mozg. Or you could peet milk with knives in it, as we used to say, and this would sharpen you up and make you ready for a bit of dirty twenty-to-one, and that was what we were peeting this evening I'm starting off the story with.

Our pockets were full of deng, so there was no real need from the point of view of crasting any more pretty polly to tolchock some old veck in an alley and viddy him swim in his blood while we counted the takings and divided by four, nor to do the ultra-violent on some shivering starry grey-haired ptitsa in a shop and go smecking off with the till's guts. But, as they say, money isn't everything.

The four of us were dressed in the height of fashion, which in those days was a pair of black very tight tights with the old jelly mould, as we called it, fitting on the crotch underneath the tights, this being to protect and also a sort of a design you could viddy clear enough in a certain light, so that I had one in the shape of a spider. Pete had a rooker (a hand, that is), Georgie had a very fancy one of a flower, and poor old Dim had a very hound-and-horny one of a clown's litso (face, that is). Dim not ever having much of an idea of things and being, beyond all shadow of a doubting thomas, the dimmest of we four. Then we wore waisty jackets without lapels but with these very big built-up shoulders ('pletchoes' we called them) which were a kind of a mockery of having real shoulders like that. Then, my brothers, we had these off-white cravats which looked like whipped-up kartoffel or spud with a sort of a design made on it with a fork. We wore our hair not too long and we had flip horrorshow boots for kicking.

'What's it going to be then, eh?'

There were three devotchkas sitting at the counter all together, but there were four of us malchicks and it was usually like one for all and all for one. These sharps were dressed in the heighth of fashion too, with purple and green and orange wigs on their gullivers, each one not costing less than three or four weeks of those sharps' wages, I should reckon, and make-up to match (rainbows round the glazzies, that is, and the rot painted very wide). Then they had long black very straight dresses, and on the groody part of them they had little badges of like silver with different malchicks' names on them – Joe and Mike and suchlike. These were supposed to be the names of the different malchicks they'd spatted with before they were fourteen. They kept looking our way and I nearly felt like saying the three of us (out of the corner of my rot, that is) should go off for a bit of pol and leave poor old Dim behind, because it would be just a matter of kupetting Dim a demi-litre of white but this time with a dollop of synthemesc in it, but that wouldn't really have been playing like the game. Dim was very very ugly and like his name, but he was a horrorshow filthy fighter and very handy with the boot.

'What's it going to be then, eh?'

The chelloveck sitting next to me, there being this long big plushy seat that ran round three walls, was well away with his glazzies glazed and sort of burbling slovos like 'Aristotle wishy washy works outing cyclamen get forficulate smartish'. He was in the land all right, well away, in orbit, and I knew what it was like, having tried it like everybody else had done, but at this time I'd got to thinking it was a cowardly sort of a veshch, O my brothers. You'd lay there after you'd drunk the old moloko and then you got the messel that everything all round you was sort of in the past. You could viddy it all right, all of it, very clear – tables, the stereo, the lights, the sharps and the malchicks – but it was like some veshch that used to be there but was not there not no more. And you were sort of hypnotized by your boot or shoe or a finger-nail as it might be, and at the same time you were sort of picked up by the old scruff and shook like you might be a cat. You got shook and shook till there was nothing left. You lost your name and your body and your self and you just didn't care, and you waited till your boot or your finger-nail got yellow, then yellower and yellower all the time. Then the lights started cracking like atomics and the boot or finger-nail or, as it might be, a bit of dirt on your trouser-bottom turned into a big big big mesto, bigger than the whole world, and you were just going to get introduced to old Bog or God when it was all over. You came back to here and now whimpering sort of, with your rot all squaring up for a boohoohoo. Now, that's very nice but very cowardly. You were not put on this earth just to get in touch with God. That sort of thing could sap all the strength and the goodness out of a chelloveck.

'What's it going to be then, eh?'

The stereo was on and you got the idea that the singer's goloss was moving from one part of the bar to another, flying up to the ceiling and then swooping down again and whizzing from wall to wall. It was Berti Laski rasping a real starry oldie called 'You Blister My Paint'. One of the three ptitsas at the counter, the one with the green wig, kept pushing her belly out and pulling it in in time to what they called the music. I could feel the knives in the old moloko starting to prick, and now I was ready for a bit of twenty-to-one. So I yelped: 'Out out out out!' like a doggie, and then I cracked this veck who was sitting next to me and well away and burbling a horrorshow crack on the ooko or earhole, but he didn't feel it and went on with his 'Telephonic hardware and when the farfarculule gets rubadubdub'. He'd feel it all right when he came to, out of the land.

'Where out?' said Georgie.

'Oh, just to keep walking,' I said, 'and viddy what turns up, O my little brothers.'

So we scatted out into the big winter nochy and walked down Marghanita Boulevard and then turned into Boothby Avenue, and there we found what we were pretty well looking for, a malenky jest to start off the evening with. There was a doddery starry schoolmaster type veck, glasses on and his rot open to the cold nochy air. He had books under his arm and a crappy umbrella and was coming round the corner from the Public Biblio, which not many lewdies used those days. You never really saw many of the older bourgeois type out after nightfall those days, what with the shortage of police and we fine young malchickiwicks about, and this prof type chelloveck was the only one walking in the whole of the street. So we goolied up to him, very polite, and I said: 'Pardon me, brother.'

He looked a malenky bit poogly when he viddied the four of us like that, coming up so quiet and polite and smiling, but he said: 'Yes? What is it?' in a very loud teacher-type goloss, as if he was trying to show us he wasn't poogly. I said:

'I see you have books under your arm, brother. It is indeed a rare pleasure these days to come across somebody that still reads, brother.'

'Oh,' he said, all shaky. 'Is it? Oh, I see.' And he kept looking from one to the other of we four, finding himself now like in the middle of a very smiling and polite square.

'Yes,' I said. 'It would interest me greatly, brother, if you would kindly allow me to see what books those are that you have under your arm. I like nothing better in this world than a good clean book, brother.'

'Clean,' he said. 'Clean, eh?' And then Pete skvatted these three books from him and handed them round real skorry. Being three, we all had one each to viddy at except for Dim. The one I had was called *Elementary Crystallography*, so I opened it up and said: 'Excellent, really first-class,' keeping turning the pages. Then I said in a very shocked type goloss: 'But what is this here? What is this filthy slovo, I blush to look at this word. You disappoint me, brother, you do really.'

'But,' he tried, 'but, but.'

'Now,' said Georgie, 'here is what I should call real dirt. There's one slovo beginning with an f and another with a c.' He had a book called *The Miracle of the Snowflake*.

'Oh,' said poor old Dim, smotting over Pete's shoulder and going too far, like he always did, 'it says here what he done to her, and there's a picture and all. Why,' he said, 'you're nothing but a filthy-minded old skitebird.'

'An old man of your age, brother,' I said, and I started to rip up the book I'd got, and the others did the same with the ones they had, Dim and Pete doing a tug-of-war with *The Rhombohedral System*. The starry prof type began to creech: 'But those are not mine, those are the property of the municipality, this is sheer wantonness and vandal work,' or some such slovos. And he tried to sort of wrest the books back off of us, which was like pathetic. 'You deserve to be taught a lesson, brother,' I said, 'that you do.' This crystal book I had was very tough-bound and hard to razrez to bits, being real starry and made in days when things were made to last like, but I managed to rip the pages up and chuck them in handfuls of like snowflakes, though big, all over this creeching old veck, and then the others did the same with theirs, old Dim just dancing about like the clown he was. 'There you are,' said Pete. 'There's the mackerel of the cornflake for you, you dirty reader of filth and nastiness.'

'You naughty old veck, you,' I said, and then we began to filly about with him. Pete held his rookers and Georgie sort of hooked his rot wide open for him and Dim yanked out his false zoobies, upper and lower. He threw these down on the pavement and then I treated them to the old boot-crush, though they were hard bastards like, being made of some new horrorshow plastic stuff. The old veck began to make sort of chumbling shooms – 'wuf waf wof' – so Georgie let go of holding his goobers apart and just let him have one in the toothless rot with his ringy fist, and that made the old veck start moaning a lot then, then out comes the blood, my brothers, real beautiful. So all we did then was to pull his outer platties off, stripping him down to his vest and long underpants (very starry; Dim smecked his head off near), and then Pete kicks him lovely in his pot, and we let him go. He went sort of staggering off, it not having been too hard of a tolchock really, going 'Oh oh oh', not knowing where or what was what really, and we had a snigger at him and then riffled through his pockets, Dim dancing round with his crappy umbrella meanwhile, but there wasn't much in them. There were a few starry letters, some of them dating right back to 1960 with 'My dearest dearest' in them and all that chepooka, and a keyring and a starry leaky pen. Old Dim gave up his umbrella dance and of course had to start reading one of the letters out loud, like to show the empty street he could read. 'My darling one,' he recited, in this very high type goloss, 'I shall be thinking of you while you are away and hope you will remember to wrap up warm when you go out at night.' Then he let out a very shoomny smeck – 'Ho ho ho' – pretending to start wiping his yahma with it. 'All right,' I said. 'Let it go, O my brothers.' In the trousers of this starry veck there was only a malenky bit of cutter (money, that is) – not more than three gollies – so we gave all his messy little coin the scatter treatment, it being hen-korm to the amount of pretty polly we had on us already. Then we smashed the umbrella and razrezzed his platties and gave them to the blowing winds, my brothers, and then we'd finished with the starry teacher type veck. We hadn't done much, I know, but that was only like the start of the evening and I make no appy polly loggies to thee or thine for that. The knives in the milk plus were stabbing away nice and horrorshow now.

The next thing was to do the sammy act, which was one way to unload some of our cutter so we'd have more of an incentive like for some shop-crasting, as well as it being a way of buying an alibi in advance, so we went into the Duke of New York on Amis Avenue and sure enough in the snug there were three or four old baboochkas peeting their black and suds on SA (State Aid). Now we were the very good malchicks, smiling good evensong to one and all, though these wrinkled old lighters started to get all shook, their veiny old rookers all trembling round their glasses, and making the suds spill on the table. 'Leave us be, lads,' said one of them, her face all mappy with being a thousand years old, 'we're only poor old women.' But we just made with the zoobies, flash flash flash, sat down, rang the bell, and waited for the boy to come. When he came, all nervous and rubbing his rookers on his grazzy apron, we ordered us four veterans – a veteran being rum and cherry brandy mixed, which was popular just then, some liking a dash of lime in it, that being the Canadian variation. Then I said to the boy:

'Give these poor old baboochkas over there a nourishing something. Large Scotchmen all round and something to take away.' And I poured my pocket of deng all over the table, and the other three did likewise, O my brothers. So double firegolds were brought in for the scared starry lighters, and they knew not what to do or say. One of them got out 'Thanks, lads,' but you could see they thought there was something dirty like coming. Anyway, they were each given a bottle of Yank General, cognac that is, to take away, and I gave money for them to be delivered each a dozen of black and suds that following morning, they to leave their stinking old cheenas' addresses at the counter. Then with the cutter that was left over we did purchase, my brothers, all the meat pies, pretzels, cheese-snacks, crisps and chocbars in that mesto, and those too were for the old sharps. Then we said: 'Back in a minoota,' and the old ptitsas were still staying: 'Thanks, lads,' and 'God bless you, boys,' and we were going out without one cent of cutter in our carmans.

'Makes you feel real dobby, that does,' said Pete. You could viddy that poor old Dim the dim didn't quite pony all that, but he said nothing for fear of being called gloopy and a domeless wonderboy. Well, we went off now round the corner to Attlee Avenue, and there was this sweets and cancers shop still open. We'd left them alone near three months now and the whole district had been very quiet on the whole, so the armed millicents or rozz patrols weren't round there much, being more north of the river these days. We put our maskies on – new jobs these were, real horrorshow, wonderfully done really; they were like faces of historical personalities (they gave you the names when you bought) and I had Disraeli, Pete had Elvis Presley, Georgie had Henry VIII and poor old Dim had a poet veck called Peebee Shelley; they were a real like disguise, hair and all, and they were some very special plastic veshch so you could roll it up when you'd done with it and hide it in your boot – then three of us went in. Pete keeping chasso without, not that there was anything to worry about out there. As soon as we launched on the shop we went for Slouse who ran it, a big portwine jelly of a veck who viddied at once what was coming and made straight for the inside where the telephone was and perhaps his well-oiled pooshka, complete with six dirty rounds. Dim was round that counter skorry as a bird, sending packets of snoutie flying and cracking over a big cut-out showing a sharp with all her zoobies going flash at the customers and her groodies near hanging out to advertise some new brand of cancers. What you could viddy then was a sort of a big ball rolling into the inside of the shop behind the curtain, this being old Dim and Slouse sort of locked in a death struggle. Then you could slooshy panting and snoring and kicking behind the curtain and veshches falling over and swearing and then glass going smash smash smash. Mother Slouse, the wife, was sort of froze behind the counter. We could tell she would creech murder given one chance, so I was round that counter very skorry and had a hold of her, and a horrorshow big lump she was too, all nuking of scent and with flipflop big bobbing groodies on her. I'd got my rooker round her rot to stop her belting out death and destruction to the four winds of heaven, but this lady doggie gave me a large foul big bite on it and it was me that did the creeching, and then she opened up beautiful with a flip yell for the millicents. Well, then she had to be tolchocked proper with one of the weights for the scales, and then a fair tap with a crowbar they had for opening cases, and that brought the red out like an old friend. So we had her down on the floor and a rip of her platties for fun and a gentle bit of the boot to stop her moaning. And, viddying her lying there with her groodies on show, I wondered should I or not, but that was for later on in the evening. Then we cleaned the till, and there was flip horrorshow takings that nochy, and we had a few packs of the very best top cancers apiece, then off we went, my brothers.

'A real big heavy great bastard he was,' Dim kept saying. I didn't like the look of Dim; he looked dirty and untidy, like a veck who'd been in a fight, which he had been, of course, but you should never *look* as though you have been. His cravat was like someone had trampled on it, his maskie had been pulled off and he had floor-dirt on his litso, so we got him in an alleyway and tidied him up a malenky bit, soaking our tashtooks in spit to cheest the dirt off. The things we did for old Dim. We were back in the Duke of New York very skorry and I reckoned by my watch we hadn't been more than ten minutes away. The starry old baboochkas were still there on the black and suds and Scotchmen we'd bought them, and we said: 'Hallo there, girlies, what's it going to be?' They started on the old 'Very kind, lads, God bless you, boys,' and so we rang the collocoll and brought a different waiter in this time and we ordered beers with rum in, being sore athirst, my brothers, and whatever the old ptitsas wanted. Then I said to the old baboochkas: 'We haven't been out of here, have we? Been here all the time, haven't we?' They all caught on real skorry and said:

'That's right, lads. Not been out of our sight, you haven't. God bless you, boys,' drinking.

Not that it mattered much, really. About half an hour went by before there was any sign of life among the millicents, and then it was only two very young rozzes that came in, very pink under their big copper's shlemmies. One said:

'You lot know anything about the happenings at Slouse's shop this night?'

'Us?' I said, innocent. 'Why, what happened?'

'Stealing and roughing. Two hospitalizations. Where've you lot been this evening?'

'I don't go for that nasty tone,' I said. 'I don't care much for these nasty insinuations. A very suspicious nature all this betokeneth, my little brothers.'

'They've been in here all night, lads,' the old sharps started to creech out. 'God bless them. there's no better lot of boys living for kindness and generosity. Been here all the time they have. Not seen them move we haven't.'

'We're only asking,' said the other young millicent. 'We've got our job to do like anyone else.' But they gave us the nasty warning look before they went out. As they were going out we handed them a bit of lip-music: brrrrzzzzrrrr. But, myself, I couldn't help a bit of disappointment at things as they were those days. Nothing to fight against really. Everything as easy as kiss-my-sharries. Still, the night was still very young.

## 2

When we got outside of the Duke of New York we viddied by the main bar's long lighted window, a burbling old pyahnitsa or drunkie, howling away at the filthy songs of his fathers and going blerp blerp in between as though it might be a filthy old orchestra in his stinking rotten guts. One veshch I could never stand was that. I could never stand to see a moodge all filthy and rolling and burping and drunk, whatever his age might be, but more especially when he was real starry like this one was. He was sort of flattened to the wall and his platties were a disgrace, all creased and untidy and covered in cal and mud and filth and stuff. So we got hold of him and cracked him with a few good horrorshow tolchocks, but he still went on singing. The song went:

> And I will go back to my darling, my darling,
> When you, my darling, are gone.

But when Dim fisted him a few times on his filthy drunkard's rot he shut up singing and started to creech: 'Go on, do me in, you bastard cowards, I don't want to live anyway, not in a stinking world like this one.' I told Dim to lay off a bit then, because it used to interest me sometimes to slooshy what some of these starry decreps had to say about life and the world. I said: 'Oh. And what's stinking about it?'

He cried out: 'It's a stinking world because it lets the young get on to the old like you done, and there's no law nor order no more.' He was creeching out loud and waving his rookers and making real horrorshow with the slovos, only the odd blurp blurp coming from his keeshkas, like something was orbiting within, or like some very rude interrupting sort of a moodge making a shoom, so that this old veck kept sort of threatening it with his fists, shouting: 'It's no world for any old man any longer, and that means that I'm not one bit scared of you, my boyos, because I'm too drunk to feel the pain if you hit me, and if you kill me I'll be glad to be dead.' We smecked and then grinned but said nothing, and then he said: 'What sort of a world is it at all? Men on the moon and men spinning round the earth like it might be midges round a lamp, and there's not no attention paid to earthly law nor order no more. So your worst you may do, you filthy cowardly hooligans.' Then he gave us some lip-music – 'Prrrrzzzzrrrr' – like we'd done to those young millicents, and then he started singing again:

> Oh dear dear land, I fought for thee
> And brought thee peace and victory –

So we cracked into him lovely, grinning all over our litsos, but he still went on singing. Then we tripped him so he laid down flat and heavy and a bucketload of beer-vomit came whooshing out. That was disgusting so we gave him the boot, one go each, and then it was blood, not song nor vomit, that came out of his filthy old rot. Then we went on our way.

It was round by the Municipal Power Plant that we came across Billyboy and his five droogs. Now in those days, my brothers, the teaming up was mostly by fours or fives, these being like auto-teams, four being a comfy number for an auto, and six being the outside limit for gang-size. Sometimes gangs would gang up so as to make like malenky armies for big night-war, but mostly it was best to roam in these like small numbers. Billyboy was something that made me want to sick just to viddy his fat grinning litso, and he always had this von of very stale oil that's been used for frying over and over, even when he was dressed in his best platties, like now. They viddied us just as we viddied them, and there was like a very quiet kind of watching each other now. This would be real, this would be proper, this would be the nozh, the oozy, the britva, not just fisties and boots. Billyboy and his droogs stopped what they were doing, which was just getting ready to perform something on a weepy young devotchka they had there, not more than ten, she creeching away but with her platties still on, Billyboy holding her by one rooker and his number-one, Leo, holding the other. They'd probably just been doing the dirty slovo part of the act before getting down to a malenky bit of ultra-violence. When they viddied us a-coming they let go of this boo-hooing little ptitsa, there being plenty more where she came from, and she ran with her thin white legs flashing through the dark, still going 'Oh oh oh'. I said, smiling very wide and droogie: 'Well, if it isn't fat stinking billygoat Billyboy in poison. How art thou, thou globby bottle of cheap stinking chip-oil? Come and get one in the yarbles, if you have any yarbles, you eunuch jelly, thou.' And then we started.

There were four of us to six of them, like I have already indicated, but poor old Dim, for all his dimness, was worth three of the others in sheer madness and dirty fighting. Dim had a real horrorshow length of oozy or chain round his waist, twice wound round, and he unwound this and began to swing it beautiful in the eyes or glazzies. Pete and Georgie had good sharp nozhes, but I for my own part had a fine starry horrorshow cut-throat britva which, at that time, I could flash and shine artistic. So there we were dratsing away in the dark, the old Luna with men on it just coming up, the stars stabbing away as it might be knives anxious to join in the dratsing. With my britva I managed to slit right down the front of one of Billyboy's droog's platties, very very neat and not even touching the plott under the cloth. Then in the dratsing this droog of Billyboy's suddenly found himself all opened up like a peapod, with his belly bare and his poor old yarbles showing, and then he got very very razdraz, waving and screaming and losing his guard and letting in old Dim with his chain snaking whisssssshhhhhhhh, so that old Dim chained him right in the glazzies, and this droog of Billyboy's went tottering off and howling his heart out. We were doing very horrorshow, and soon we had Billyboy's number-one down underfoot, blinded with old Dim's chain and crawling and howling about like an animal, but with one fair boot on the gulliver he was out and out and out.

Of the four of us Dim, as usual, came out the worst in point of looks, that is to say his litso was all bloodied and his platties a dirty mess, but the others of us were still cool and whole. It was stinking fatty Billyboy I wanted now, and there I was dancing about with my britva like I might be a barber on board a ship on a very rough sea, trying to get in at him with a few fair slashes on his unclean oily litso. Billyboy had a nozh, a long flick-type, but he was a malenky bit too slow and heavy in his movements to vred anyone really bad. And, my brothers, it was real satisfaction to me to waltz – left two three, right two three – and carve left cheeky and right cheeky, so that like two curtains of blood seemed to pour out at the same time, one on either side of his fat filthy oily snout in the winter starlight. Down this blood poured in like red curtains, but you could viddy Billyboy felt not a thing, and he went lumbering on like a filthy fatty bear, poking at me with his nozh.

Then we slooshied the sirens and knew the millicents were coming with pooshkas pushing out of the police-auto-windows at the ready. That little weepy devotchka had told them, no doubt, there being a box for calling the rozzes not too far behind the Muni Power Plant. 'Get you soon, fear not,' I called, 'stinking billygoat. I'll have your yarbles off lovely.' Then off they ran, slow and panting, except for Number One Leo out snoring on the ground, away north towards the river, and we went the other way. Just round the next turning was an alley, dark and empty and open at both ends, and we rested there, panting fast then slower, then breathing like normal. It was like resting between the feet of two terrific and very enormous mountains, these being the flatblocks, and in the windows of all of the flats you could viddy like blue dancing light. This would be the telly. Tonight was what they called a worldcast, meaning that the same programme was being viddied by everybody in the world that wanted to, that being mostly the middle-aged middle-class lewdies. There would be some big famous stupid comic chelloveck or black singer, and it was all being bounced off the special telly satellites in outer space, my brothers. We waited panting, and we could slooshy the sirening millicents going east, so we knew we were all right now. But poor old Dim kept looking up at the stars and planets and the Luna with his rot wide open like a kid who'd never viddied any such things before, and he said:

'What's on them, I wonder. What would be up there on things like that?'

I nudged him hard, saying: 'Come, gloopy bastard as thou art.

Think thou not on them. There'll be life like down here most likely, with some getting knifed and others doing the knifing. And now, with the nochy still molodoy, let us be on our way, O my brothers.' The others smecked at this, but poor old Dim looked at me serious, then up again at the stars and the Luna. So we went on our way down the alley, with the worldcast blueing on on either side. What we needed now was an auto, so we turned left coming out of the alley, knowing right away we were in Priestly Place as soon as we viddied the big bronze statue of some starry poet with an apey upper lip and a pipe stuck in a droopy old rot. Going north we came to the filthy old Filmdrome, peeling and dropping to bits through nobody going there much except malchicks like me and my droogs, and then only for a yell or a razrez or a bit of in-out-in-out in the dark. We could viddy from the poster on the Filmdrome's face, a couple of fly-dirtied spots trained on it, that there was the usual cowboy riot, with the archangels on the side of the US marshal six-shooting at the rustlers out of hell's fighting legions, the kind of hound-and-horny veshch put out by Statefilm in those days. The autos parked by the sinny weren't all that horrorshow, crappy starry veshches most of them, but there was a newish Durango 95 that I thought might do. Georgie had one of these polyclefs, as they called them, on his keyring, so we were soon aboard – Dim and Pete at the back, puffing away lordly at their cancers – and I turned on the ignition and started her up and she grumbled away real horrorshow, a nice warm vibraty feeling grumbling all through your guttiwuts. Then I made with the noga, and we backed out lovely, and nobody viddied us take off.

We fillied round what was called the backtown for a bit, scaring old vecks and cheenas that were crossing the roads and zigzagging after cats and that. Then we took the road west. There wasn't much traffic about, so I kept pushing the old noga through the floorboards near, and the Durango 95 ate up the road like spaghetti. Soon it was winter trees and dark, my brothers, with a country dark, and at one place I ran over something big with a snarling toothy rot in the head-lamps, then it screamed and squelched under and old Dim at the back near laughed his gulliver off – 'Ho ho ho' – at that. Then we saw one young malchick with his sharp, lubbilubbing under a tree, so we stopped and cheered at them, then we bashed into them both with a couple of half-hearted tolchocks, making them cry, and on we went. What we were after now was the old surprise visit. That was a real kick and good for smecks and lashings of the ultra-violent. We came at last to a sort of a village, and just outside this village was a small sort of a cottage on its own with a bit of a garden. The Luna was well up now, and we could viddy this cottage fine and clear as I eased up and put the brake on, the other three giggling like bezoomny, and we could viddy the name on the gate of this cottage veshch was HOME, a gloomy sort of a name. I got out of the auto, ordering my droogs to shush their giggles and act like serious, and I opened this malenky gate and walked up to the front door. I knocked nice and gentle and nobody came, so I knocked a bit more and this time I could slooshy somebody coming, then a bolt drawn, then the door inched open an inch or so, then I could viddy this one glazz looking out at me and the door was on a chain. 'Yes? Who is it?' It was a sharp's goloss, a youngish devotchka by her sound, so I said in a very refined manner of speech, a real gentleman's goloss:

'Pardon, madam, most sorry to disturb you, but my friend and me were out for a walk, and my friend has taken bad all of a sudden with a very troublesome turn, and he is out there on the road dead out and groaning. Would you have the goodness to let me use your telephone to telephone for an ambulance?'

'We haven't a telephone,' said this devotchka. 'I'm sorry, but we haven't. You'll have to go somewhere else.' From inside this malenky cottage I could slooshy the clack clack clacky clack clack clackity clackclack of some veck typing away, and then the typing stopped and there was this chelloveck's goloss calling: 'What is it, dear?'

'Well,' I said, 'could you of your goodness please let him have a cup of water? It's like a faint, you see. It seems as though he's passed out in a sort of a fainting fit.'

The devotchka sort of hesitated and then said: 'Wait.' Then she went off, and my three droogs had got out of the auto quiet and crept up horrorshow stealthy, putting their maskies on now, then I put mine on, then it was only a matter of me putting in the old rooker and undoing the chain, me having softened up this devotchka with my gent's goloss, so that she hadn't shut the door like she should have done, us being strangers of the night. The four of us then went roaring in, old Dim playing the shoot as usual with his jumping up and down and singing out dirty slovos, and it was a nice malenky cottage, I'll say that. We all went smecking into the room with a light on, and there was this devotchka sort of cowering, a young pretty bit of sharp with real horrorshow groodies on her, and with her was this chelloveck who was her moodge, youngish too with horn-rimmed otchkies on him, and on a table was a typewriter and all papers scattered everywhere, but there was one little pile of paper like that must have been what he'd already typed, so here was another intelligent type bookman type like that we'd fillied with some hours back, but this one was a writer not a reader. Anyway, he said:

'What is this? Who are you? How dare you enter my house without permission.' And all the time his goloss was trembling and his rookers too. So I said:

'Never fear. If fear thou hast in thy heart, O brother, pray banish it forthwith.' Then Georgie and Pete went out to find the kitchen, while old Dim waited for orders, standing next to me with his rot wide open. 'What is this, then?' I said, picking up the pile like of typing from off of the table, and the horn-rimmed moodge said, dithering:

'That's just what I want to know. What is this? What do you want? Get out at once before I throw you out.' So poor old Dim, masked like Peebee Shelley, had a good loud smeck at that, roaring like some animal.

'It's a book,' I said. 'It's a book what you are writing.' I made the old goloss very coarse. 'I have always had the strongest admiration for them as can write books.' Then I looked at its top sheet, and there was the name – A CLOCKWORK ORANGE – and I said: 'That's a fair gloopy title. Who ever heard of a clockwork orange?' Then I read a malenky bit out loud in a sort of very high type preaching goloss: ' – The attempt to impose upon man, a creature of growth and capable of sweetness, to ooze juicily at the last round the bearded lips of God, to attempt to impose, I say, laws and conditions appropriate to a mechanical creation, against this I raise my sword-pen – ' Dim made the old lip-music at that and I had to smeck myself. Then I started to tear up the sheets and scatter the bits over the floor, and this writer moodge went sort of bezoomny and made for me with his zoobies clenched and showing yellow and his nails ready for me like claws. So that was old Dim's cue and he went grinning and going er er and a a a for this veck's dithering rot, crack crack, first left fistie then right, so that our dear old droog the red – red vino on tap and the same in all places, like it's put out by the same big firm – started to pour and spot the nice clean carpet and the bits of this book that I was still ripping away at, razrez razrez. All this time this devotchka, his loving and faithful wife, just stood like froze by the fireplace, and then she started letting out little malenky creeches, like in time to the like music of old Dim's fisty work. Then Georgie and Pete came in from the kitchen, both munching away, though with their maskies on, you could do that with them on and no trouble, Georgie with like a cold leg of something in one rooker and half a loaf of kleb with a big dollop of maslo on it in the other, and Pete with a bottle of beer frothing its gulliver off and a horrorshow rookerful of like plum cake. They went haw haw haw, viddying old Dim dancing round and fisting the writer veck so that the writer veck started to platch like his life's work was ruined, going boo hoo hoo with a very square bloody rot, but it was haw haw haw in a muffled eater's way and you could see bits of what they were eating. I didn't like that, it being dirty and slobbery, so I said:

'Drop that mounch. I gave no permission. Grab hold of this veck here so he can viddy all and not get away.' So they put down their fatty pishcha on the table among all the flying paper and they clopped over to the writer veck whose horn-rimmed otchkies were cracked but still hanging on, with old Dim still dancing round and making ornaments shake on the mantelpiece (I swept them all off then and they couldn't shake no more, little brothers) while he fillied with the author of *A Clockwork Orange*, making his litso all purple and dripping away like some very special sort of a juicy fruit. 'All right, Dim,' I said. 'Now for the other veshch, Bog help us all.' So he did the strong-man on the devotchka, who was still creech creech creeching away in very horrorshow four-in-a-bar, locking her rookers from the back, while I ripped away at this and that and the other, the others going haw haw haw still, and real good horrorshow groodies they were that then exhibited their pink glazzies, O my brothers, while I untrussed and got ready for the plunge. Plunging, I could slooshy cries of agony and this writer bleeding veck that Georgie and Pete held on to nearly got loose howling bezoomny with the filthiest of slovos that I already knew and others he was making up. Then after me it was right old Dim should have his turn, which he did in a beasty snorty howly sort of a way with his Peebee Shelley maskie taking no notice, while I held on to her. Then there was a changeover, Dim and me grabbing the slobbering writer veck who was past struggling really, only just coming out with slack sort of slovos like he was in the land in a milk-plus bar, and Pete and Georgie had theirs. Then there was like quiet and we were full of like hate, so smashed what was left to be smashed – typewriter, lamp, chairs – and Dim, it was typical of old Dim, watered the fire out and was going to dung on the carpet, there being plenty of paper, but I said no. 'Out out out out,' I howled. The writer veck and his zheena were not really there, bloody and torn and making noises. But they'd live.

So we got into the waiting auto and I left it to Georgie to take the wheel, me feeling that malenky bit shagged, and we went back to town, running over odd squealing things on the way.

# 3

We yeckated back townwards, my brothers, but just outside, not far from what they called the Industrial Canal, we viddied the fuel needle had like collapsed, like our own ha ha ha needles had, and the auto was coughing kashl kashl kashl. Not to worry overmuch, though, because a rail station kept flashing blue – on off on off – just near. The point was whether to leave the auto to be sobiratted by the rozzes or, us feeling like in a hate and murder mood, to give it a fair tolchock into the starry waters for a nice heavy loud plesk before the death of the evening. This latter we decided on, so we got out and, the brakes off, all four tolchocked it to the edge of the filthy water that was like treacle mixed with human hole products, then one good horrorshow tolchock and in she went. We had to dash back for fear of the filth splashing on our platties, but splussshhhh and glolp she went, down and lovely. 'Farewell, old droog,' called Georgie, and Dim obliged with a clowny great guff – 'Huh huh huh huh.' Then we made for the station to ride the one stop to Center, as the middle of the town was called. We paid our fares nice and polite and waited gentlemanly and quiet on the platform, old Dim fillying with the slot machines, his carmans being full of small malenky coin, and ready if need be to distribute chocbars to the poor and starving, though there was none such about, and then the old espresso rapido came lumbering in and we climbed aboard, the train looking to be near empty. To pass the three-minute ride we fillied about with what they called the upholstery, doing some nice horrorshow tearing-out of the seats' guts and old Dim chaining the okno till the glass cracked and sparkled in the winter air, but we were all feeling that big shagged and fagged and fashed, it having been an evening of some small energy expenditure, my brothers, only Dim, like the clowny animal he was, full of the joys-of, but looking all dirtied over and too much von of sweat on him, which was one thing I had against old Dim.

We got out at Center and walked slow back to the Korova Milkbar, all going yawwwww a malenky bit and exhibiting to moon and star and lamplight our back fillings, because we were still only growing malchicks and had school in the daytime, and when we got into the Korova we found it fuller than when we'd left earlier on. But the chelloveck that had been burbling away, in the land, on white and synthemesc or whatever, was still on at it, going: 'Urchins of deadcast in the way-ho-hay glill platonic time weatherborn.' It was probable that this was his third or fourth lot that evening, for he had that pale inhuman look, like he'd become a *thing*, and like his litso was really a piece of chalk carved. Really, if he wanted to spend so long in the land, he should have gone into one of the private cubies at the back and not stayed in the big mesto, because here some of the malchickies would filly about with him a malenky bit, though not too much because there were powerful bruiseboys hidden away in the old Korova who could stop any riot. Anyway, Dim squeezed in next to this veck and, with his big clown's yawp that showed his hanging grape, he stabbed this veck's foot with his own large filthy sabog. But the veck, my brothers, heard nought, being now all above the body.

It was nadsats milking and coking and fillying around (nadsats were what we used to call the teens), but there were a few of the more starry ones, vecks and cheenas alike (but not of the bourgeois, never them) laughing and govoreeting at the bar. You could tell from their barberings and loose platties (big stringy sweaters mostly) that they'd been on rehearsals at the TV studios round the corner. The devotchkas among them had these very lively litsos and wide big rots, very red, showing a lot of teeth, and smecking away and not caring about the wicked world one whit. And then the disc on the stereo twanged off and out (it was Johnny Zhivago, a Russky koshka, singing 'Only Every Other Day'), and in the like interval, the short silence before the next one came on, one of these devotchkas – very fair and with a big smiling red rot and in her late thirties I'd say – suddenly came with a burst of singing, only a bar and a half and as though she was like giving an example of something they'd all been govoreeting about. and it was like for a moment, O my brothers, some great bird had flown into the milkbar, and I felt all the little malenky hairs on my plott standing endwise and the shivers crawling up like slow malenky lizards and then down again. Because I knew what she sang. It was from an opera by Friedrich Gitterfenster called *Das Bettzeug*, and it was the bit where she's snuffing it with her throat cut, and the slovos are 'Better like this maybe'. Anyway, I shivered.

But old Dim, as soon as he'd slooshied this dollop of song like a lomtick of redhot meat plonked on your plate, let off one of his vulgarities, which in this case was a lip-trump followed by a dog-howl followed by two fingers pronging twice at the air followed by a clowny guffaw. I felt myself all of a fever and like drowning in redhot blood, slooshying and viddying Dim's vulgarity, and I said: 'Bastard. Filthy drooling mannerless bastard.' Then I leaned across Georgie, who was between me and horrible Dim, and fisted Dim skorry on the rot. Dim looked very surprised, his rot open, wiping the krovvy off of his goober with his rook and in turn looking surprised at the red flowing krovvy and at me. 'What for did you do that for?' he said in his ignorant way. Not many viddied what I'd done, and those that viddied cared not. The stereo was on again and was playing a very sick electronic guitar veshch. I said:

'For being a bastard with no manners and not the dook of an idea how to comport yourself publicwise, O my brother.'

Dim put on a hound-and-horny look of evil, saying: 'I don't like you should do what you done then. And I'm not your brother no more and wouldn't want to be.' He'd taken a big snotty tashtook from his pocket and was mopping the red flow puzzled, keeping on looking at it frowning as if he thought that blood was for other vecks and not for him. It was like he was singing blood to make up for his vulgarity when that devotchka was singing music. But that devotchka was smecking away ha ha ha now with her droogs at the bar, her red rot working and her zoobies ashine, not having noticed Dim's filthy vulgarity. It was me really Dim had done wrong to. I said:

'If you don't like this and you wouldn't want that, then you know what to do, little brother.' Georgie said, in a sharp way that made me look:

'All right. Let's not be starting.'

'That's clean up to Dim,' I said. 'Dim can't go on all his jeezny being as a little child.' And I looked sharp at Georgie. Dim said, and the red krovvy was easing its flow now:

'What natural right does he have to think he can give the orders and tolchock me whenever he likes? Yarbles is what I say to him, and I'd chain his glazzies out soon as look.'

'Watch that,' I said, as quiet as I could with the stereo bouncing all over the walls and ceiling and the in-the-land veck beyond Dim getting loud now with his 'Spark nearer, ultoptimate', I said: 'Do watch that, O Dim, if to continue to be on live thou dost wish.'

'Yarbles,' said Dim, sneering, 'great bolshy yarblockos to you. What you done then you had no right. I'll meet you with chain or nozh or britva any time, not having you aiming tolchocks at me reasonless, it stands to reason I won't have it.'

'A nozh scrap any time you say,' I snarled back. Pete said:

'Oh now, don't, both of you malchicks. Droogs, aren't we? It isn't right droogs should behave thiswise. See, there are some loose-lipped malchicks over there smecking at us, leering like. We mustn't let ourselves down.'

'Dim,' I said, 'has got to learn his place. Right?'

'Wait,' said Georgie. 'What's all this about place? This is the first I ever hear about lewdies learning their place.'

Pete said: 'If the truth is known, Alex, you shouldn't have given old Dim that uncalled-for tolchock. I'll say it once and no more. I say it with all respect, but if it had been me you'd given it to you'd have to answer. I say no more.' And he drowned his litso in his milk-glass.

I could feel myself getting all razdraz inside, but I tried to cover it, saying calm: 'There has to be a leader. Discipline there has to be. Right?' None of them skazatted a word or nodded even. I got more razdraz inside, calmer out. 'I,' I said, 'have been in charge long now. We are all droogs, but somebody has to be in charge. Right? Right?' They all like nodded, wary like. Dim was osooshing the last of the krovvy off. It was Dim who said now:

'Right, right. Doobidoob. A bit tired, maybe, everybody is. Best not to say more.' I was surprised and just that malenky bit poogly to sloosh Dim govoreeting that wise. Dim said: 'Bedways is rightways now, so best we go homeways. Right?' I was very surprised. The other two nodded, going right right right. I said:

'You understand about that tolchock on the rot, Dim. It was the music, see. I get all bezoomny when any veck interferes with a ptitsa singing, as it might be. Like that then.'

'Best we go off homeways and get a bit of spatchka,' said Dim. 'A long night for growing malchicks. Right?' Right right nodded the other two. I said:

'I think it best we go home now. Dim has made a real horrorshow suggestion. If we don't meet day-wise, O my brothers, well then – same time same place tomorrow?'

'Oh yes,' said Georgie. 'I think that can be arranged.'

'I might,' said Dim, 'be just that malenky bit late. But same place and near same time tomorrow surely.' He was still wiping at his goober, though no krovvy flowed any longer now. 'And,' he said, 'it's to be hoped there won't be no more of them singing ptitsas in here.'

Then he gave his old Dim guff, a clowny big hohohohoho. It seemed like he was too dim to take much offence.

So off we went our several ways, me belching arrrrgh on the cold coke I'd peeted. I had my cut-throat britva handy in case any of Billyboy's droogs should be around near the flatblock waiting, or for that matter any of the other bandas or gruppas or shaikas that from time to time were at war with one. Where I lived was with my dadda and mum in the flats of Municipal Flatblock 18A, between Kingsley Avenue and Wilsonsway. I got to the big main door with no trouble, though I did pass one young malchick sprawling and creeching and moaning in the gutter, all cut about lovely, and saw in the lamplight also streaks of blood here and there like signatures, my brothers, of the night's fillying. And too I saw just by 18A a pair of devotchka's neezhnies doubtless rudely wrenched off in the heat of the moment, O my brothers. And so in. In the hallway was the good old municipal painting on the walls – vecks and ptitsas very well developed, stern in the dignity of labour, at workbench and machine with not one stitch of platties on their well-developed plotts. But of course some of the malchicks living in 18A had, as was to be expected, embellished and decorated the said big painting with handy pencil and ballpoint, adding hair and stiff rods and dirty ballooning slovos out of the dignified rots of these nagoy (bare, that is) cheenas and vecks. I went to the lift, but there was no need to press the electric knopka to see if it was working or not, because it had been tolchocked real horrorshow this night, the metal doors all buckled, some feat of rare strength indeed, so I had to walk the ten floors up. I cursed and panted climbing, being tired in plott if not so much in brain. I wanted music very bad this evening, that singing devotchka in the Korova having perhaps started me off. I wanted like a big feast of it before getting my passport stamped, my brothers, at sleep's frontier and the stripy shest lifted to let me through.

I opened the door of 10–8 with my own little klootch, and inside our malenky quarters all was quiet, the pee and em both being in sleepland, and mum had laid out on the table on malenky bit of supper – a couple of lomticks of tinned spongemeat with a shive or so of kleb and butter, a glass of the old cold moloko. Hohoho, the old moloko, with no knives or synthemesc or drencrom in it. How wicked, my brothers, innocent milk must always seem to me now. Still, I drank and ate growling, being more hungry than I thought at first, and I got fruit-pie from the larder and tore chunks off it to stuff into my greedy rot. Then I tooth-cleaned and clicked, cleaning out the old rot with my yahzick or tongue, then I went into my own little room or den, easing off my platties as I did so. Here was my bed and my stereo, pride of my jeezny, and my discs in their cupboard, and banners and flags on the wall, these being like remembrances of my corrective school life since I was eleven, O my brothers, each one shining and blazoned with name or number: SOUTH 4; METRO CORSKOL BLUE DIVISION; THE BOYS OF ALPHA.

The little speakers of my stereo were all arranged round the room, on ceiling, walls, floor, so, lying on my bed slooshying the music, I was like netted and meshed in the orchestra. Now what I fancied first tonight was this new violin concerto by the American Geoffrey Plautus, played by Odysseus Choerilos with the Macon (Georgia) Philharmonic, so I slid it from where it was neatly filed and switched on and waited.

Then, brothers, it came. Oh, bliss, bliss and heaven. I lay all nagoy to the ceiling, my gulliver on my rookers on the pillow, glazzies closed, rot open in bliss, slooshying the sluice of lovely sounds. Oh, it was gorgeousness and gorgeosity made flesh. The trombones crunched redgold under my bed, and behind my gulliver the trumpets three-wise silverflamed, and there by the door the timps rolling through my guts and out again crunched like candy thunder. Oh, it was wonder of wonders. And then, a bird of like rarest spun heavenmetal, or like silvery wine flowing in a spaceship, gravity all nonsense now, came the violin solo above all the other strings, and those strings were like a cage of silk round my bed. Then flute and oboe bored, like worms of like platinum, into the thick thick toffee gold and silver. I was in such bliss, my brothers. Pee and em in their bedroom next door had learnt now not to knock on the wall with complaints of what they called noise. I had taught them. Now they would take sleep-pills. Perhaps, knowing the joy I had in my night music, they had already taken them. As I slooshied, my glazzies tight shut to shut in the bliss that was better than any synthemesc Bog or God, I knew such lovely pictures. There were vecks and ptitsas, both young and starry, lying on the ground screaming for mercy, and I was smecking all over my rot and grinding my boot in their litsos. And there were devotchkas ripped and creeching against walls and I plunging like a shlaga into them, and indeed when the music, which was one movement only, rose to the top of its big highest tower, then, lying there on my bed with glazzies tight shut and rookers behind my gulliver, I broke and spattered and cried aaaaaaah with the bliss of it. And so the lovely music glided to its glowing close.

After that I had lovely Mozart, the Jupiter, and there were new pictures of different litsos to be ground and splashed, and it was after this that I thought I would have just one last disc only before crossing the border, and I wanted something starry and strong and very firm, so it was J. S. Bach I had, the Brandenburg Concerto just for middle and lower strings. And, slooshying with different bliss than before, I viddied again this name on the paper I'd razrezzed that night, a long time ago it seemed, in that cottage called HOME. The name was about a clockwork orange. Listening to the J. S. Bach, I began to pony better what that meant now, and I thought, slooshying away to the brown gorgeousness of the starry German master, that I would like to have tolchecked them both harder and ripped them to ribbons on their own floor.

## 4

The next morning I woke up at oh eight oh oh hours, my brothers, and as I still felt shagged and fagged and fashed and bashed and my glazzies were stuck together real horrorshow with sleepglue, I thought I would not go to school. I thought how I would have a malenky bit longer in the bed, an hour or two say, and then get dressed nice and easy, perhaps even having a splosh about in the bath, make toast for myself and slooshy the radio or read the gazetta, all on my oddy knocky. And then in the afterlunch I might perhaps, if I still felt like it, itty off to the old skolliwoll and see what was vareeting in that great seat of gloopy useless learning, O my brothers. I heard my papapa grumbling and trampling and then ittying off to the dyeworks where he rabbited, and then my mum called in in a very respectful goloss as she did now I was growing up big and strong:

'It's gone eight, son. You don't want to be late again.'

So I called back: 'A bit of a pain in my gulliver. Leave us be and I'll try to sleep it off and then I'll be right as dodgers for this after.' I slooshied her give a sort of a sigh and she said:

'I'll put your breakfast in the oven then, son. I've got to be off myself now.' Which was true, there being this law for everybody not a child nor with child nor ill to go out rabbiting. My mum worked at one of the Statemarts, as they called them, filling up the shelves with tinned soup and beans and all that cal. So I slooshied her clank a plate in the gas-oven like and then she was putting her shoes on and then getting her coat from behind the door and then sighing again, then she said: 'I'm off now, son.' But I let on to be back in sleepland and then I did doze off real horrorshow, and I had a queer and very real like sneety, dreaming for some reason of my droog Georgie. In this sneety he'd got like very much older and very sharp and hard and was govoreeting about discipline and obedience and how all the malchicks under his control had to jump hard at it and throw up the old salute like being in the army, and there was me in line like the rest saying yes sir and no sir, and then I viddied clear that Georgie had these stars on his pletchoes and he was like a general. And then he brought in old Dim with a whip, and Dim was a lot more starry and grey and had a few zoobies missing as you could see when he let out a smeck, viddying me, and then my droog Georgie said, pointing like at me: 'That man has filth and cal all over his platties,' and it was true. Then I creeched: 'Don't hit, please don't, brothers,' and started to run. And I was running in like circles and Dim was after me, smecking his gulliver off, cracking with the old whip, and each time I got a real horrorshow tolchock with this whip there was like a very loud electric bell ringringringing, and this bell was like a sort of a pain too.

Then I woke up real skorry, my heart going bap bap bap, and of course there was really a bell going brrrrr, and it was our front-door bell. I let on that nobody was at home, but this brrrrr still ittied on, and then I heard a goloss shouting through the door: 'Come on then, get out of it, I know you're in bed.' I recognized the goloss right away. It was the goloss of P. R. Deltoid (a real gloopy nazz, that one) what they called my Post-Corrective Adviser, an overworked veck with hundreds on his books. I shouted right right right, in a goloss of like pain, and I got out of bed and attired myself, O my brothers, in a very lovely over-gown of like silk, with designs of like great cities all over this over-gown. Then I put my nogas into very comfy woolly toofles, combed my luscious glory, and was ready for P. R. Deltoid. When I opened up he came shambling in looking shagged, a battered old shlapa on his gulliver, his raincoat filthy. 'Ah, Alex boy,' he said to me. 'I met your mother, yes. She said something about a pain somewhere. Hence not at school, yes.'

'A rather intolerable pain in the head, brother, sir,' I said in my gentleman's goloss. 'I think it should clear by this afternoon.'

'Or certainly by this evening, yes,' said P. R. Deltoid. 'The evening is the great time, isn't it, Alex boy? Sit,' he said, 'sit, sit,' as though this was his domy and me his guest. And he sat in this starry rocking-chair of my dad's and began rocking, as if that was all he had come for. I said:

'A cup of the old chai, sir? Tea, I mean.'

'No time,' he said. And he rocked, giving me the old glint under frowning brows, as if with all the time in the world. 'No time, yes,' he said, gloopy. So I put the kettle on. Then I said:

'To what do I owe the extreme pleasure? Is anything wrong, sir?'

'Wrong?' he said, very skorry and sly, sort of hunched looking at me but still rocking away. Then he caught sight of an advert in the gazetta, which was on the table – a lovely smecking young ptitsa with her groodies hanging out to advertise, my brothers, the Glories of the Jugoslav Beaches. Then, after sort of eating her up in two swallows, he said: 'Why should you think in terms of there being anything wrong? Have you been doing something you shouldn't, yes?'

'Just a manner of speech,' I said, 'sir.'

'Well,' said P. R. Deltoid, 'it's just a manner of speech from me to you that you watch out, little Alex, because next time, as you very well know, it's not going to be the corrective school any more. Next time it's going to be the barry place and all my work ruined. If you have no consideration for your horrible self you at least might have some for me, who have sweated over you. A big black mark, I tell you in confidence, for every one we don't reclaim, a confession of failure for every one of you that ends up in the stripy hole.'

'I've been doing nothing I shouldn't, sir,' I said. 'The millicents have nothing on me, brother, sir I mean.'

'Cut out this clever talk about millicents,' said P. R. Deltoid very weary, but still rocking. 'Just because the police have not picked you up lately doesn't, as you very well know, mean you've not been up to some nastiness. There was a bit of a fight last night, wasn't there? There was a bit of shuffling with nozhes and bike-chains and the like. One of a certain fat boy's friends was ambulanced off late from near the Power Plant and hospitalized, cut about very unpleasantly, yes. Your name was mentioned. The word has got through to me by the usual channels. Certain friends of yours were named also. There seems to have been a fair amount of assorted nastiness last night. Oh, nobody can prove anything about anybody, as usual. But I'm warning you, little Alex, being a good friend to you as always, the one man in this sore and sick community who wants to save you from yourself.'

'I appreciate all that, sir,' I said, 'very sincerely.'

'Yes, you do, don't you?' he sort of sneered. 'Just watch it, that's all, yes. We know more than you think, little Alex.' Then he said, in a goloss of great suffering, but still rocking away: 'What gets into you all? We study the problem and we've been studying it for damn well near a century, yes, but we get no further with our studies. You've got a good home here, good loving parents, you've got not too bad of a brain. Is it some devil that crawls inside you?'

'Nobody's got anything on me, sir,' I said. 'I've been out of the rookers of the millicents for a long time now.'

'That's just what worries me,' sighed P. R. Deltoid. 'A bit too long of a time to be healthy. You're about due now by my reckoning. That's why I'm warning you, little Alex, to keep your handsome young proboscis out of the dirt, yes. Do I make myself clear?'

'As an unmuddied lake, sir,' I said. 'Clear as an azure sky of deepest summer. You can rely on me, sir.' And I gave him a nice zooby smile.

But when he'd ookadeeted and I was making this very strong pot of chai, I grinned to myself over this veshch that P. R. Deltoid and his droogs worried about. All right, I do bad, what with crasting and tolchocks and carves with the britva and the old in-out-in-out, and if I get loveted, well, too bad for me, O my little brothers, and you can't run a country with every chelloveck comporting himself in my manner of the night. So if I get loveted and it's three months in this mesto and another six in that, and then, as P. R. Deltoid so kindly warns, next time, in spite of the great tenderness of my summers, brothers, it's the great unearthly zoo itself, well, I say: 'Fair, but a pity, my lords, because I just cannot bear to be shut in. My endeavour shall be, in such future as stretches out its snowy and lilywhite arms to me before the nozh overtakes or the blood spatters its final chorus in twisted metal and smashed glass on the highroad, to not get loveted again.' Which is fair speeching. But, brothers, this biting of their toe-nails over what is the *cause* of badness is what turns me into a fine laughing malchick. They don't go into the cause of *goodness*, so why the other shop? If lewdies arc good that's because they like it, and I wouldn't ever interfere with their pleasures, and so of the other shop. And I was patronizing the other shop. More, badness is of the self, the one, the you or me on our oddy knockies, and that self is made by old Bog or God and is his great pride and radosty. But the not-self cannot have the bad, meaning they of the government and the judges and the schools cannot allow the bad because they cannot allow the self. And is not our modern history, my brothers, the story of brave malenky selves fighting these big machines? I am serious with you, brothers, over this. But what I do I do because I like to do.

So now, this smiling winter morning, I drink this very strong chai with moloko and spoon after spoon after spoon of sugar, me having a sladky tooth, and I dragged out of the oven the breakfast my poor old mum had cooked for me. It was an egg fried, that and no more, but I made toast and ate egg and toast and jam, smacking away at it while I read the gazetta. The gazetta was the usual about ultra-violence and bank robberies and strikes and footballers making everybody paralytic with fright by threatening to not play next Saturday if they did not get higher wages, naughty malchickiwicks as they were. Also there were more space-trips and bigger stereo TV screens and offers of free packets of soapflakes in exchange for the labels on soup-tins, amazing offer for one week only, which made me smeck. And there was a bolshy big article on Modern Youth (meaning me, so I gave the old bow, grinning like bezoomny) by some very clever bald chelloveck. I read this with care, my brothers, slurping away at the old chai, cup after tass after chasha, crunching my lomticks of black toast dipped in jammiwam and eggiweg. This learned veck said the usual veshches, about no parental discipline, as he called it, and the shortage of real horrorshow teachers who would lambast bloody beggary out of their innocent poops and make them go boohoohoo for mercy. All this was gloopy and made me smeck, but it was like nice to go on knowing one was making the news all the time, O my brothers. Every day there was something about Modern Youth, but the best veshch they ever had in the old gazetta was by some starry pop in a doggy collar who said that in his considered opinion and he was govoreeting as a man of Bog IT WAS THE DEVIL THAT WAS ABROAD and was like ferreting his way into like young innocent flesh, and it was the adult world that could take the responsibility for this with their wars and bombs and nonsense. So that was all right. So he knew what he talked of, being a Godman. So we young innocent malchicks could take no blame. Right right right.

When I'd gone erk erk a couple of razzes on my full innocent stomach, I started to get out day platties from my wardrobe, turning the radio on. There was music playing, a very nice malenky string quartet, my brothers, by Claudius Birdman, one that I knew well. I had to have a smeck, though, thinking of what I'd viddied once in one of these like articles on Modern Youth, about how Modern Youth would be better off if A Lively Appreciation Of The Arts could be like encouraged. Great Music, it said, and Great Poetry would like quieten Modern Youth down and make Modern Youth more Civilized. Civilized my syphilised yarbles. Music always sort of sharpened me up, O my brothers, and made me like feel like old Bog himself, ready to make with the old donner and blitzen and have vecks and ptitsas creeding away in my ha ha power. And when I'd cheested up my litso and rookers a bit and done dressing (my day platties were like

student-wear: the old blue pantalonies with sweater with A for Alex)
I thought here at least was time to itty off to the disc-bootick (and
cutter too, my pockets being full of pretty polly) to see about this
long-promised and long-ordered stereo Beethoven Number Nine (the
Choral Symphony, that is), recorded on Masterstroke by the Esh
Sham Sinfonia under L. Muhaiwir. So out I went, brothers.

The day was very different from the night. The night belonged to
me and my droogs and all the rest of the nadsats, and the starry
bourgeois lurked indoors drinking in the gloopy worldcasts, but the
day was for the starry ones, and there always seemed to be more
rozzes or millicents about during the day, too. I got the autobus from
the corner and rode to Center, and then I walked back to Taylor
Place, and there was the disc-bootick I favoured with my inestimable
custom, O my brothers. It had the gloopy name of MELODIA, but
it was a real horrorshow mesto and skorry, most times, at getting the
new recordings. I walked in and the only other customers were two
young ptitsas sucking away at ice-sticks (and this, mark, was dead
cold winter and sort of shuffling through the new pop-discs – Johnny
Burnaway, Stash Kroh, The Mixers, Lay Quiet Awhile With Ed And
Id Molotov, and all the rest of that cal). These two ptitsas couldn't
have been more than ten, and they too, like me, it seemed, evidently,
had decided to take the morning off from the old skolliwoll. They
saw themselves, you could see, as real grown-up devotchkas already,
what with the old hip-swing when they saw your Faithful Narrator,
brothers, and padded groodies and red all ploshed on their goobers.
I went up to the counter, making with the polite zooby smile at old
Andy behind it (always polite himself, always helpful, a real horrorshow
type of a veck, though bald and very very thin). He said:

'Aha, I know what you want, I think. Good news, good news. It
has arrived.' And with like big conductor's rookers beating time he
went to get it. The two young ptitsas started giggling, as they will at
that age, and I gave them a like cold glazzy. Andy was back real skorry,
waving the great shiny white sleeve of the Ninth, which had on it,
brothers, the frowning beetled like thunderbolted litso of Ludwig
van himself. 'Here,' said Andy. 'Shall we give it the trial spin?' But I
wanted it back home on my stereo to slooshy on my oddy knocky,

greedy as hell. I fumbled out the deng to pay and one of the little ptitsas said:

'Who you getten, bratty? What biggy, what only?' These young devotchkas had their own like way of govoreeting. 'The Heaven Seventeen? Luke Sterne? Goggly Gogol?' And both giggled, rocking and hippy. Then an idea hit me and made me near fall over with the anguish and ecstasy of it, O my brothers, so I could not breathe for near ten seconds. I recovered and made with my new-clean zoobies and said:

'What you got back home, little sisters, to play your fuzzy warbles on?' Because I could viddy the discs they were buying were these teeny pop veshches. 'I bet you got little save tiny portable like picnic spinners.' And they sort of pushed their lower lips out at that. 'Come with uncle,' I said, 'and hear all proper. Hear angel trumpets and devil trombones. You are invited.' And I like bowed. They giggled again and one said:

'Oh, but we're so hungry. Oh, but we could so eat.' The other said: 'Yah, she can say that, can't she just.' So I said:

'Eat with uncle. Name your place.'

Then they viddied themselves as real sophistoes, which was like pathetic, and started talking in big-lady golosses about the Ritz and the Bristol and the Hilton and Il Ristorante Granturco. But I stopped that with 'Follow uncle,' and I led them to the Pasta Parlour just round the corner and let them fill their innocent young litsos on spaghetti and sausages and cream-puffs and banana-splits and hot choc-sauce, till I near sicked with the sight of it, brothers, lunching but frugally off a cold ham-slice and a growling dollop of chilli. These two young ptitsas were much alike, though not sisters. They had the same ideas or lack of, and the same colour hair – a like dyed strawy. Well, they would grow up real today. Today I would make a day of it. No school this afterlunch, but education certain, Alex as teacher. Their names, they said, were Marty and Sonietta, bezoomy enough and in the heighth of their childish fashion, so I said:

'Righty right, Marty and Sonietta. Time for the big spin. Come.' When we were outside on the cold street they thought they would not go by autobus, oh no, but by taxi, so I gave them the humour, though with a real horrorshow ingrin, and I called a taxi from the rank near Center. The driver, a starry whiskery veck in very stained platties, said:

'No tearing up, now. No nonsense with them seats. Just re-upholstered they are.' I quieted his gloopy fears and off we spun to Municipal Flatblock 18A, these two bold little ptitsas giggling and whispering. So, to cut all short, we arrived. O my brothers, and I led the way up to 10–8, and they panted and smecked away the way up, and then they were thirsty, they said, so I unlocked the treasure-chest in my room and gave these ten-year-young devotchkas a real horrorshow Scotchman apiece, though well filled with sneezy pins-and-needles soda. They sat on my bed (yet unmade) and leg-swung, smecking and peeting their highballs, while I spun their like pathetic malenky discs through my stereo. Like peeting some sweet scented kid's drink, that was, in like very beautiful and lovely and costly gold goblets. But they went oh oh oh and said, 'Swoony' and 'Hilly' and other weird slovos that were the heighth of fashion in that youth group. While I spun this cal for them I encouraged them to drink and have another, and they were nothing loath, O my brothers. So by the time their pathetic pop-discs had been twice spun each (there were two: 'Honey Nose', sung by Ike Yard, and 'Night After Day After Night', moaned by two horrible yarbleless like eunuchs whose names I forget) they were getting near the pitch of like young ptitsa's hysterics, what with jumping all over my bed and me in the room with them.

What was actually done that afternoon there is no need to describe, brothers, as you may easily guess all. Those two were unplattied and smecking fit to crack in no time at all, and they thought it the bolshiest fun to viddy old Uncle Alex standing there all nagoy and pan-handled, squirting the hypodermic like some bare doctor, then giving myself the old jab of growling jungle-cat secretion in the rooker. Then I pulled the lovely Ninth out of its sleeve, so that Ludwig van was now nagoy too, and I set the needle hissing on to the last movement, which was all bliss. There it was then, the bass strings like govoreeting away from under my bed at the rest of the orchestra, and then the male human goloss coming in and telling them all to be joyful, and then the lovely blissful tune all about Joy being a glorious spark like of heaven, and then I felt the old tigers leap in me and then I leapt on these two young ptitsas. This time they thought nothing fun and stopped creeching with high mirth, and had to submit to the strange and weird desires of Alexander the Large which, what with the Ninth and the hypo jab, were choodessny and zammechat and very demanding, O my brothers. But they were both very very drunken and could hardly feel very much.

When the last movement had gone round for the second time with all the banging and creeching about Joy Joy Joy Joy, then these two young ptitsas were not acting the big lady sophisto no more. They were like waking up to what was being done to their malenky persons and saying that they wanted to go home and like I was a wild beast. They looked like they had been in some big bitva, as indeed they had, and were all bruised and pouty. Well, if they would not go to school they must still have their education. And education they had had. They were creeching and going ow ow ow as they put their platties on, and they were like punchipunching me with their teeny fists as I lay there dirty and nagoy and fair shagged and fagged on the bed. This young Sonietta was creeching: 'Beast and hateful animal. Filthy horror.' So I let them get their things together and get out, which they did, talking about how the rozzes should be got on to me and all that cal. Then they were going down the stairs and I dropped off to sleep, still with the old Joy Joy Joy Joy crashing and howling away.

# 5

What happened, though, was that I woke up late (near seven-thirty by my watch) and, as it turned out, that was not so clever. You can viddy that everything in this wicked world counts. You can pony that one thing always leads to another. Right right right. My stereo was no longer on about Joy and I Embrace Ye O Ye Millions, so some veck had dealt it the off, and that would be either pee or em, both of them now being quite clear to the slooshying in the living-room and, from the clink clink of plates and slurp slurp of peeting tea from cups,

at their tired meal after the day's rabb[...]
the other. The poor old. The pitiable starr[...]
and looked out, in guise of loving only son, to [...]

'Hi hi hi, there. A lot better after the day's res[...]
evening work to earn that little bit.' For that's what t[...]
believed I did these days. 'Yum, yum, mum. Any of that f[...]
was like some frozen pie that she'd unfroze and then warmed u[...]
it looked not so very appetitish, but I had to say what I said. Da[...]
looked at me with a not-so-pleased suspicious like look but said
nothing, knowing he dared not, and mum gave me a tired like little
smeck, to thee fruit of my womb my only son sort of. I danced to the
bathroom and had a real skorry cheest all over, feeling dirty and gluey,
then back to my den for the evening's platties. Then, shining, combed,
brushed and gorgeous, I sat to my lomtick of pie. Papapa said:

'Not that I want to pry, son, but where exactly is it you go to work
of evenings?'

'Oh,' I chewed, 'it's mostly odd things, helping like. Here and there,
as it might be.' I gave him a straight dirty glazzy, as to say to mind
his own and I'd mind mine. 'I never ask for money, do I? Not money
for clothes or for pleasures? All right, then, why ask?'

My dad was like humble mumble chumble. 'Sorry, son,' he said.
'But I get worried sometimes. Sometimes I have dreams. You can
laugh if you like, but there's a lot in dreams. Last night I had this
dream with you in it and I didn't like it one bit.'

'Oh?' He had gotten me interessovatted now, dreaming of me
like that. I had like a feeling I had had a dream, too, but I could
not remember proper what. 'Yes?' I said, stopping chewing my gluey
pie.

'It was vivid,' said my dad. 'I saw you lying on the street and you
had been beaten by other boys. These boys were like the boys you
used to go around with before you were sent to that last Corrective
School.'

'Oh?' I had an in-grin at that, papapa believing I had really reformed
or believing he believed. And then I remembered my own dream,
which was a dream of that morning, of Georgie giving his general's
orders and old Dim smecking around toothless as he wielded the

e told. 'Never worry about
said. 'Fear not. He canst

pless in your blood and you
osites, so I had another quiet
ll the deng out of my carmans
I. I said:

I earned last night. But perhaps
he snug somewhere for you and

on't go out much now. We daren't
go ou   hat they are. Young hooligans and
so on. Still, th  her home a bottle of something
tomorrow.' And he scoop his ill-gotten pretty into his trouser
carmans, mum being at the cheesting of the dishes in the kitchen.
And I went out with loving smiles all round.

When I got to the bottom of the stairs of the flatblock I was
somewhat surprised. I was more than that. I opened my rot like wide
in the old stony gapes. They had come to meet me. They were waiting
by the all scrawled-over municipal wall-painting of the nagoy dignity
of labour, bare vecks and cheenas stern at the wheels of industry, like
I said, with all this dirt pencilled from their rots by naughty malchicks.
Dim had a big thick stick of black greasepaint and was tracing filthy
slovos real big over our municipal painting and doing the old Dim
guff – wuh huh huh – while he did it. But he turned round when
Georgie and Pete gave me the well hello, showing their shining droogy
zoobies, and he horned out: 'He are here, he have arrived, hooray,'
and did a clumsy turnitoe bit of dancing.

'We got worried,' said Georgie. 'There we were awaiting and peeting
away at the old knify moloko, and you might have been like offended
by some veshch or other, so round we come to your abode. That's
right, Pete, right?'

'Oh, yes, right,' said Pete.

'Appy polly loggies,' I said careful. 'I had something of a pain in
the gulliver so had to sleep. I was not wakened when I gave orders
for wakening. Still, here we all are, ready for what the old nochy offers,

yes?' I seemed to have picked up that yes? from P. R. Deltoid, my Post-Corrective Adviser. Very strange.

'Sorry about the pain,' said Georgie, like very concerned. 'Using the gulliver too much like, maybe. Giving orders and discipline and such, perhaps. Sure the pain is gone? Sure you'll not be happier going back to the bed?' And they all had a bit of a malenky grin.

'Wait,' I said. 'Let's get things nice and sparkling clear. This sarcasm, if I may call it such, does not become you, O my little friends. Perhaps you have been having a bit of a quiet govoreet behind my back, making your own little jokes and such-like. As I am your droog and leader, surely I am entitled to know what goes on, eh? Now then, Dim, what does that great big horsy gape of a grin portend?' For Dim had his rot open in a sort of bezoomy soundless smeck. Georgie got in very skorry with:

'All right, no more picking on Dim, brother. That's part of the new way.'

'New way?' I said. 'What's this about a new way? There's been some very large talk behind my sleeping back and no error. Let me slooshy more.' And I sort of folded my rookers and leaned comfortable to listen against the broken banister-rail, me being still higher than them, droogs as they called themselves, on the third stair.

'No offence, Alex,' said Pete, 'but we wanted to have things more democratic like. Not like you like saying what to do and what not all the time. But no offence,'

George said: 'Offence is neither here nor elsewhere. It's the matter of who has ideas. What ideas has he had?' And he kept his very bold glazzies turned full on me. 'It's all the small stuff, malenky veshches like last night. We're growing up, brothers.'

'More,' I said, not moving. 'Let me slooshy more.'

'Well,' said Georgie, 'if you must have it, have it then. We itty round, shop-crasting and the like, coming out with a pitiful rookerful of cutter each. And there's Will the English in the Muscleman coffee mesto saying he can fence anything that any malchick cares to try to crast. The shiny stuff, the ice,' he said, still with these like cold glazzies on me. 'The big big big money is available is what Will the English says.'

'So,' I said, very comfortable out but real razdraz within. 'Since when have you been consorting and comporting with Will the English?'

'Now and again,' said Georgie, 'I get around all on my oddy knocky. Like last Sabbath for instance. I can live my own jeezny, droogie, right?'

I didn't care for any of this, my brothers. 'And what will you do,' I said, 'with the big big big deng or money as you so highfaluting call it? Have you not every veshch you need? If you need an auto you pluck it from the trees. If you need pretty polly you take it. Yes? Why this sudden shilarny for being the big bloated capitalist?'

'Ah,' said Georgie, 'you think and govoreet sometimes like a little child.' Dim went huh huh huh at that. 'Tonight,' said Georgie, 'we pull a mansize crast.'

So my dream had told truth, then. Georgie the general saying what we should do and what not do, Dim with the whip as mindless grinning bulldog. But I played with care, with great care, the greatest, saying, smiling: 'Good. Real horrorshow. Initiative comes to them as wait. I have taught you much, little droogie. Now tell me what you have in mind, Georgie-boy.'

'Oh,' said Georgie, cunning and crafty in his grin, 'the old moloko-plus first, would you not say? Something to sharpen us up, boy, but you especially, we having the start on you.'

'You have govoreeted my thoughts for me,' I smiled away. 'I was about to suggest the dear old Korova. Good good good. Lead, little Georgie.' And I made with a like deep bow, smiling like bezoomny but thinking all the time. But when we got into the street I viddied that thinking is for the gloopy ones and that the oomny ones use like inspiration and what Bog sends. For now it was lovely music that came to my aid. There was an auto ittying by and it had its radio on, and I could just slooshy a bar or so of Ludwig van (it was the Violin Concerto, last movement), and I viddied right at once what to do. I said, in like a thick deep goloss: 'Right, Georgie, now,' and I whished out my cut-throat britva. Georgie said: 'Uh?' but he was skorry enough with his nozh, the blade coming sloosh out of the handle, and we were on to each other. Old Dim said: 'Oh no, not right that isn't, and made to uncoil the chain round his tally, but Pete said, putting his rooker firm on old Dim: 'Leave them. It's right like that.' So then Georgie and Your Humble did the old quiet cat-stalk, looking for openings, knowing each other's style a bit too horrorshow really, Georgie now and then going lurch lurch with his shining nozh but not no wise connecting. And all the time lewdies passed by and viddied all this but minded their own, it being perhaps a common street-sight. But then I counted odin dva tree and went ak ak ak with the britva, though not at litso or glazzies but at Georgie's nozh-holding rooker and, my little brothers, he dropped. He did. He dropped his nozh with a tinkle tankle on the hard winter sidewalk. I had just ticklewickled his fingers with my britva, and there he was looking at the malenky dribble of krovvy that was redding out in the lamplight. 'Now,' I said, and it was me that was starting, because Pete had given old Dim the soviet not to uncoil the oozy from round his tally and Dim had taken it, 'now, Dim, let's thou and me have all this now, shall us?' Dim went, 'Aaaaaaarhgh,' like some bolshy bezoomny animal, and snaked out the chain from his waist real horrorshow and skorry, so you had to admire. Now the right style for me here was to keep low like in frog-dancing to protect litso and glazzies, and this I did, brothers, so that poor old Dim was a malenky bit surprised, him being accustomed to the straight face-on lash lash lash. Now I will say that he whished me horrible on the back so that it stung like bezoomny, but that pain told me to dig in skorry once and for all and be done with old Dim. So I swished with the britva at his left noga in its very tight tight and I slashed two inches of cloth and drew a malenky drop of krovvy to make Dim real bezoomny. Then while he went hauwwww hauwww hauwww like a doggie I tried the same style as for Georgie, banking all on one move – up, cross, cut – and I felt the britva go just deep enough in the meat of old Dim's wrist and he dropped his snaking oozy yelping like a little child. Then he tried to drink in all the blood from his wrist and howl at the same time, and there was too much krovvy to drink and he went bubble bubble bubble, the red like fountaining out lovely, but not for very long. I said:

'Right, my droogies, now we should know. Yes, Pete?'

'I never said anything,' said Pete. 'I never govoreeted one slovo. Look, old Dim's bleeding to death.'

'Never,' I said. 'One can die but once. Dim died before he was born. That red red krovvy will soon stop.' Because I had not cut into the like main cables. And I myself took a clean tashtook from my carman to wrap round poor old dying Dim's rooker, howling and moaning as he was, and the krovvy stopped like I said it would, O my brothers. So they knew now who was master and leader, sheep, thought I.

It did not take long to quieten these two wounded soldiers down in the snug of the Duke of New York, what with large brandies (bought with their own cutter, me having given all to my dad, and a wipe with tashtooks dipped in the water-jug. The old ptitsas we'd been so horrorshow to last night were there again, going, 'Thanks, lads' and 'God bless you, boys' like they couldn't stop, though we had not repeated the old sammy act with them. But Pete said: 'What's it to be, girls?' and bought black and suds for them, him seeming to have a fair amount of pretty polly in his carmans, so they were on louder than ever with their 'God bless and keep you all, lads' and 'We'd never split on you, boys' and 'The best lads breathing, that's what you are.' At last I said to Georgie:

'Now we're back to where we were, yes? Just like before and all forgotten, right?'

'Right right right,' said Georgie. But old Dim still looked a bit dazed and he even said: 'I could have got that big bastard, see, with my oozy, only some veck got in the way,' as though he'd been dratsing not with me but with some other malchick. I said:

'Well, Georgieboy, what did you have in mind?'

'Oh,' said Georgie, 'not tonight. Not this nochy, please.'

'You're a big strong chelloveck,' I said, 'like us all. We're not little children, are we, Georgieboy? What, then, didst thou in thy mind have?'

'I could have chained his glazzies real horrorshow,' said Dim, and the old baboochkas were still on with their 'Thanks, lads.'

'It was this house, see,' said Georgie. 'The one with the two lamps outside. The one with the gloopy name, like.'

'What gloopy name?'

'The Mansion or the Manse or some such piece of gloop. Where this very starry ptitsa lives with her cats and all these very starry valuable veshches.'

'Such as?'

'Gold and silver and like jewels. It was Will the English who like said.'

'I viddy,' I said. 'I viddy horrorshow.' I knew where he meant – Oldtown, just beyond Victoria Flatblock. Well, the real horrorshow leader knows always when like to give and show generous to his like unders. 'Very good, Georgie,' I said. 'A good thought, and one to be followed. Let us at once itty.' And as we were going out the old baboochkas said: 'We'll say nothing, lads. Been here all the time you have, boys.' So I said: 'Good old girls. Back to buy more in ten minutes.' And so I led my three droogs out to my doom.

# 6

Just past the Duke of New York going east was offices and then there was the starry beat-up biblio and then was the bolshy flatblock called Victoria Flatblock after some victory or other, and then you came to the like starry type houses of the town in what was called Oldtown. You got some of the real horrorshow ancient domies here, my brothers, with starry lewdies living in them, thin old barking like colonels with sticks and old ptitsas who were widows and deaf starry damas with cats who, my brothers, had felt not the touch of any chelloveck in the whole of their pure like jeeznies. And here, true, there were starry veshches that would fetch their share of cutter on the tourist market – like pictures and jewels and other starry pre-plastic cal of that type. So we came nice and quiet to this domy called the Manse, and there were globe lights outside on iron stalks, like guarding the front door on each side, and there was a light like dim on in one of the rooms on the ground level, and we went to a nice patch of street dark to watch through the window what was ittying on. This window had iron bars in front of it, like the house was a prison, but we could viddy nice and clear what was ittying on.

What was ittying on was that this starry ptitsa, very grey in the

voloss and with a very liny like litso, was pouring the old moloko
from a milk-bottle into saucers and then setting these saucers down
on the floor, so you could tell there were plenty of mewing kots and
koshkas writhing about down there. And we could viddy one or two,
great fat scoteenas, jumping up on to the table with their rots open
going mare mare mare. And you could viddy this old baboochka
talking back to them, govoreeting in like scoldy language to her
pussies. In the room you could viddy a lot of old pictures on the walls
and starry very elaborate clocks, also some like vases and ornaments
that looked starry and dorogoy. Georgie whispered: 'Real horrorshow
deng to be gotten for them, brothers. Will the English is real anxious.'
Pete said: 'How in?' Now it was up to me, and skorry, before Georgie
started telling us how. 'First veshch,' I whispered, 'is to try the regular
way, the front. I will go very polite and say that one of my droogs has
had a like funny fainting turn on the street. Georgie can be ready to
show, when she opens, thatwise. Then to ask for water or to phone
the doc. Then in easy.' Georgie said:

'She may not open.' I said:

'We'll try it, yes?' And he sort of shrugged his pletchoes, making
with a frog's rot. So I said to Pete and old Dim: 'You two droogies
get either side of the door. Right?' They nodded in the dark right right
right. 'So,' I said to Georgie, and I made bold straight for the front
door. There was a bellpush and I pushed, and brrrrrrr brrrrr sounded
down the hall inside. A like sense of slooshying followed, as though
the ptitsa and her koshkas all had their ears back at the brrrrr brrrrrr,
wondering. So I pushed the old zvonock a malenky bit more urgent.
I then bent down to the letter-slit and called through in a refined like
goloss: 'Help, madam, please. My friend has just had a funny turn on
the street. Let me phone a doctor, please.' Then I could viddy a light
being put on in the hall, and then I could hear the old baboochka's
nogas going flip flap in flip-flap slippers to nearer the front door, and
I got the idea, I don't know why, that she had a big fat pussycat under
each arm. Then she called out in a very surprising deep like goloss:

'Go away. Go away or I shoot.' Georgie heard that and wanted to
giggle. I said, with like suffering and urgency in my gentleman's goloss:

'Oh, please help, madam. My friend's very ill.'

'Go away,' she called. 'I know your dirty tricks, making me open the door and then buy things I don't want. Go away, I tell you.' That was real lovely innocence, that was. 'Go away,' she said again, 'or I'll set my cats on to you.' A malenky bit bezoomny she was, you could tell that, through spending her jeezny all on her oddy knocky. Then I looked up and I viddied that there was a sash-window above the front door and that it would be a lot more skorry to just do the old pletcho climb and get in that way. Else there'd be this argument all the long nochy. So I said:

'Very well, madam. If you won't help I must take my suffering friend elsewhere.' And I winked my droogies all away quiet, only me crying out: 'All right, old friend, you will surely meet some good samaritan some place other. This old lady perhaps cannot be blamed for being suspicious with so many scoundrels and rogues of the night about. No, indeed not.' Then we waited again in the dark and I whispered: 'Right, Return to the door. Me stand on Dim's pletchoes. Open that window and me enter, droogies. Then to shut up that old ptitsa and open up for all. No trouble.' For I was like showing who was leader and the chelloveck with the ideas. 'See,' I said. 'Real horrorshow bit of stonework over that door, a nice hold for my nogas.' They viddied all that, admiring perhaps I thought, and said and nodded Right right right in the dark.

So back tiptoe to the door. Dim was our heavy strong malchick and Pete and Georgie like heaved me up on to Dim's bolshy manly pletchoes. All this time, O thanks to worldcasts on the gloopy TV and, more, lewdies' night-fear through lack of night-police, dead lay the street. Up there on Dim's pletchoes I viddied that this stonework above the door would take my boots lovely. I kneed up, brothers, and there I was. The window, as I had expected, was closed, but I outed with my britva and cracked the glass of the window smart with the bony handle thereof. All the time below my droogies were hard breathing. So I put in my rooker through the crack and made the lower half of the window sail up open silver-smooth and lovely. And I was, like getting into the bath, in. And there were my sheep down below, their rots open as they looked up, O brothers.

I was in bumpy darkness, with beds and cupboards and bolshy

heavy stoolies and piles of boxes and books about. But I strode manful towards the door of the room I was in, seeing a like crack of light under it. The door went squeeeeeeeeeeeak and then I was on a dusty corridor with other doors. All this waste, brothers, meaning all these rooms and but one starry sharp and her pussies, but perhaps the kots and koshkas had like separate bedrooms, living on cream and fish-heads like royal queens and princes. I could hear the like muffled goloss of this old ptitsa down below saying: 'Yes yes yes, that's it,' but she would be govoreeting to these mewing sidlers going maaaaaaa for more moloko. Then I saw the stairs going down to the hall and I thought to myself that I would show these fickle and worthless droogs of mine that I was worth the whole three of them and more. I would do all on my oddy knocky. I would perform the old ultra-violence on the starry ptitsa and on her pusspots if need be, then I would take fair rookerfuls of what looked like real polezny stuff and go waltzing to the front door and open up showering gold and silver on my waiting droogs. They must learn all about leadership.

So down I ittied, slow and gentle, admiring in the stairwell grahzny pictures of old time – devotchkas with long hair and high collars; the like country with trees and horses, the holy bearded veck all nagoy hanging on a cross. There was a real musty von of pussies and pussy-fish and starry dust in this domy, different from the flatblocks. And then I was downstairs and I could viddy the light in this front room where she had been doling moloko to the kots and koshkas. More, I could viddy these great overstuffed scoteenas going in and out with their tails waving and like rubbing themselves on the door-bottom. On a like big wooden chest in the dark hall I could viddy a nice malenky statue that shone in the light of the room, so I crasted this for my own self, it being like a young thin devotchka standing on one noga with her rookers out, and I could see this was made of silver. So I had this when I ittied into the lit-up room, saying: 'Hi hi hi. At last we meet. Our brief govoreet through the letter-hole was not, shall we say, satisfactory, yes? Let us admit not, oh verily not, you stinking starry old sharp.' And I like blinked in the light at this room and the old ptitsa in it. It was full of kots and koshkas all crawling to and fro over the carpet, with bits of fur floating in the lower air, and these fat scoteenas were all different shapes and colours, black, white, tabby, ginger, tortoise-shell, and of all ages, too, so that there were kittens fillying about with each other and there were pussies full-grown and there were real dribbling starry ones very bad-tempered. Their mistress, this old ptitsa, looked at me fierce like a man and said:

'How did you get in? Keep your distance, you villainous young toad, or I shall be forced to strike you.'

I had a real horrorshow smeck at that, viddying that she had in her veiny rooker a crappy wood walking-stick which she raised at me threatening. So, making with my shiny zoobies, I ittied a bit nearer to her, taking my time, and on the way I saw on a like sideboard a lovely little veshch, the loveliest malenky veshch any malchick fond of music like myself could ever hope to viddy with his own two glazzies, for it was like the gulliver and pletchoes of Ludwig van himself, what they call a bust, a like stone veshch with stone long hair and blind glazzies and the big flowing cravat. I was off for that right away, saying: 'Well, how lovely and all for me.' But ittying towards it with my glazzies like full on it and my greedy rooker held out, I did not see the milk saucers on the floor and into one I went and sort of lost balance. 'Whoops,' I said, trying to steady, but this old ptitsa had come up behind me very sly and with great skorriness for her age and then she went crack crack on my gulliver with her bit of a stick. So I found myself on my rookers and knees trying to get up and saying: 'Naughty, naughty naughty.' And then she was going crack crack crack again, saying: 'Wretched little slummy bedbug, breaking into *real* people's houses.' I didn't like this crack crack eegra, so I grasped hold of one end of her stick as it came down again and then she lost her balance and was trying to steady herself against the table, but then the table-cloth came off with a milk-jug and a milk-bottle going all drunk then scattering white splosh in all directions, then she was down on the floor grunting, going: 'Blast you, boy, you shall suffer.' Now all the cats were getting spoogy and running and jumping in a like cat-panic, and some were blaming each other, hitting out cat-tolchocks with the old lapa and ptaaaaa and grrrrr and kraaaaark. I got up on to my nogas, and there was this nasty vindictive starry forella with her wattles ashake and grunting as she like tried to lever herself up from the floor, so I gave her a malenky fair kick in the litso, and she didn't like that, crying: 'Waaaaah,' and you could viddy her veiny mottled litso going purplewurple where I'd landed the old noga.

As I stepped back from the kick I must have like trod on the tail of one of these dratsing creeching pusspots, because I slooshied a gromky yauuuuuuuuw and found that like fur and teeth and claws had like fastened themselves round my leg, and there I was cursing away and trying to shake it off holding this silver malenky statue in one rooker and trying to climb over this old ptitsa on the floor to reach lovely Ludwig van in frowning like stone. And then I was into another saucer brimful of creamy moloko and near went flying again, the whole veshch really a very humorous one if you could imagine it sloochatting to some other veck and not to Your Humble Narrator. And then the starry ptitsa on the floor reached over all the dratsing yowling pusscats and grabbed at my noga, still going 'Waaaaah' at me, and, my balance being a bit gone, I went really crash this time, on to sploshing moloko and skriking koshkas, and the old forella started to fist me on the litso, both of us being on the floor, creeching: 'Thrash him, beat him, pull out his finger-nails, the poisonous young beetle,' addressing her pusscats only, and then, as if like obeying the starry old ptitsa, a couple of koshkas got on to me and started scratching like bezoomny. So then I got real bezoomny myself, brothers, and hit out at them, but this baboochka said: 'Toad, don't touch my kitties,' and like scratched my litso. So then I screeched: 'You filthy old soomka', and upped with the little malenky like silver statue and cracked her a fine fair tolchock on the gulliver and that shut her up real horrorshow and lovely.

Now as I got up from the floor among all the craking kots and koshkas what should I slooshy but the shoom of the old police-auto siren in the distance, and it dawned on me skorry that the old forella of the pusscats had been on the phone to the millicents when I thought she'd been govoreeting to the mewlers and mowlers, her having got her suspicions skorry on the boil when I'd rung the old zvonock pretending for help. So now, slooshying this fearsome shoom of the rozzvan, I belted for the front door and had a rabbiting time undoing all the locks and chains and bolts and other protective veshches. Then I got it open, and who should be on the doorstep but old Dim, me just being able to viddy the other two of my so-called droogs belting off. 'Away,' I creeched to Dim. 'The rozzes are coming.' Dim said: 'You stay to meet them huh huh huh,' and then I viddied that he had his oozy out, and then he upped with it and it snaked whishhh and he chained me gentle and artistic like on the glazlids, me just closing them up in time. Then I was howling around trying to viddy with this howling great pain, and Dim said: 'I don't like you should do what you done, old droogy. Not right it wasn't to get on to me like the way you done, brat.' And then I could slooshy his bolshy lumpy boots beating off, him going huh huh huh into the darkmans, and it was only about seven seconds after that I slooshied the millicent-van draw up with a filthy great dropping siren-howl, like some bezoomny animal snuffing it. I was howling too and like yawing about and I banged my gulliver smack on the hall-wall, my glazzies being tight shut and the juice astream from them, very agonizing. So there I was like groping in the hallway as the millicents arrived. I couldn't viddy them, of course, but I could slooshy and damn near smell the von of the bastards, and soon I could feel the bastards as they got rough and did the old twist-arm act, carrying me out. I could also slooshy one millicent goloss saying from like the room I'd come out of with all the kots and koshkas in it: 'She's been nastily knocked but she's breathing,' and there was loud mewing all the time.

'A real pleasure this is,' I heard another millicent goloss say as I was tolchocked very rough and skorry into the auto. 'Little Alex all to our own selves.' I creeched out:

'I'm blind, Bog bust and bleed you, you grahzny bastards.'

'Language, language,' like smecked a goloss, and then I got a like backhand tolchock with some ringy rooker or other full on the rot. I said:

'Bog murder you, you vonny stinking bratchnies. Where are the others? Where are my stinking traitorous droogs? One of my cursed grahzny bratties chained me on the glazzies. Get them before they get away. It was all their idea, brothers. They like forced me to do it. I'm innocent, Bog butcher you.' By this time they were all having like a good smeck at me with the heighth of like callousness, and they'd tolchocked me into the back of the auto, but I still kept on about these so-called droogs of mine and then I viddied it would be no good, because they'd all be back now in the snug of the Duke of New York forcing black and suds and double Scotchmen down the unprotesting gorloes of those stinking starry ptitsas and they saying: 'Thanks, lads. God bless you, boys. Been here all the time you have, lads. Not been out of our sight you haven't.'

All the time we were sirening off to the rozz-shop, me being wedged between two millicents and being given the odd thump and malenky tolchock by these smecking bullies. Then I found I could open up my glazlids a malenky bit and viddy like through all tears a kind of steamy city going by, all the lights like having run into one another. I could viddy now through smarting glazzies these two smecking millicents at the back with me and the thin-necked driver and the fat-necked bastard next to him, this one having a sarky like govoreet at me, saying: 'Well, Alex boy, we all look forward to a pleasant evening together, don't we not?' I said:

'How do you know my name, you stinking vonny bully? May Bog blast you to hell, grahzny bratchny as you are, you sod.' So they all had a smeck at that and I had my ooko like twisted by one of these stinking millicents at the back with me. The fat-necked not-driver said:

'Everybody knows little Alex and his droogs. Quite a famous young boy our Alex has become.'

'It's those others,' I creeched. 'Georgie and Dim and Pete. No droogs of mine, the bastards.'

'Well,' said the fat-neck, 'you've got the evening in front of you to tell the whole story of the daring exploits of those young gentlemen and how they led poor little innocent Alex astray.' Then there was the shoom of another like police siren passing this auto but going the other way.

'Is that for those bastards?' I said. 'Are they being picked up by you bastards?'

'That,' said fat-neck, 'is an ambulance. Doubtless for your old lady victim, you ghastly wretched scoundrel.'

'It was all their fault,' I creeched, blinking my smarting glazzies. 'The bastards will be peeting away in the Duke of New York. Pick them up blast you, you vonny sods.' And then there was more smecking and another malenky tolchock, O my brothers, on my poor smarting rot. And then we arrived at the stinking rozz-shop and they helped me get out of the auto with kicks and pulls and they tolchocked me up the steps and I knew I was going to get nothing like fair play from these stinky grahzny bratchnies, Bog blast them.

# 7

They dragged me into this very bright-lit whitewashed cantora, and it had a strong von that was a mixture of like sick and lavatories and beery rots and disinfectant, all coming from the barry places near by. You could hear some of the plennies in their cells cursing and singing and I fancied I could slooshy one belting out:

> 'And I will go back to my darling, my darling.
> When you, my darling, are gone.'

But there were the golosses of millicents telling them to shut it and you could even slooshy the zvook of like somebody being tolchocked real horrorshow and going owwwwwwwwww, and it was like the goloss of a drunken starry ptitsa, not a man. With me in this cantora were four millicents, all having a good loud peet of chai, a big pot of it being on the table and they sucking and belching away over their dirty bolshy mugs. They didn't offer me any. All that they gave me, my brothers, was a crappy starry mirror to look into, and indeed I was not your handsome young Narrator any longer but a real strack of a sight, my rot swollen and my glazzies all red and my nose bumped a bit also. They all had a real horrorshow smeck when they viddied my like dismay, and one of them said: 'Love's young nightmare like.' And then a top millicent came in with like stars on his pletchoes to show he was high high high, and he viddied me and said: 'Hm.' So then they started. I said:

'I won't say one single solitary slovo unless I have my lawyer here.

I know the law, you bastards.' Of course they all had a good gromky smeck at that and the stellar top millicent said:

'Righty right, boys, we'll start off by showing him that we know the law, too, but that knowing the law isn't everything.' He had a like gentleman's goloss and spoke in a very weary sort of a way, and he nodded with a like droogy smile at one very big fat bastard. This big fat bastard took off his tunic and you could viddy he had a real big starry pot on him, then he came up to me not too skorry and I could get the von of the milky chai he'd been peeting when he opened his rot in a like very tired leery grin at me. He was not too well shaved for a rozz and you could viddy like patches of dried sweat on his shirt under the arms, and you could get this von of like earwax from him as he came close. Then he clenched his stinking red rooker and let me have it right in the belly, which was unfair, and all the other millicents smecked their gullivers off at that, except the top one and he kept on with this weary like bored grin. I had to lean against the white-washed wall so that all the white got on to my platties, trying to drag the old breath back and in great agony, and then I wanted to sick up the gluey pie I'd had before the start of the evening. But I couldn't stand that sort of veshch, sicking all over the floor, so I held it back. Then I saw that this fatty bruiseboy was turning to his millicent droogs to have a real horrorshow smeck at what he'd done, so I raised my right noga and before they could creech at him to watch out I'd kicked him smart and lovely on the shin. And he creeched murder, hopping around.

But after that they all had a turn, bouncing me from one to the other like some very weary bloody ball, O my brothers, and fisting me in the yarbles and the rot and the belly and dealing out kicks, and then at last I had to sick up on the floor and, like some real bezoomny veck, I even said: 'Sorry, brothers, that was not the right thing at all. Sorry sorry sorry.' But they handed me starry bits of gazetta and made me wipe it, then they made me make with the sawdust. And then they said, almost like dear old droogs, that I was to sit down and we'd all have a quiet like govoreet. And then P. R. Deltoid came in to have a viddy, his office being in the same building, looking very tired and grahzny, to say: 'So it's happened, Alex boy, yes? Just as I thought it would. Dear dear dear, yes.' Then he turned to the millicents to say: 'Evening, inspector. Evening, sergeant. Evening, evening, all. Well, this is the end of the line for me, yes. Dear dear, this boy does look messy, doesn't he? Just look at the state of him.'

'Violence makes violence,' said the top millicent in a very holy type goloss. 'He resisted his lawful arresters.'

'End of the line, yes,' said P. R. Deltoid again. He looked at me with very cold glazzies like I had become a thing and was no more a bleeding very tired battered chelloveck. 'I suppose I'll have to be in court tomorrow.'

'It wasn't me, brother, sir,' I said, a malenky bit weepy. 'Speak up for me, sir, for I'm not so bad. I was led on by the treachery of the others, sir.'

'Sings like a linnet,' said the top rozz, sneery. 'Sings the roof off lovely, he does that.'

'I'll speak,' said cold P. R. Deltoid. 'I'll be there tomorrow, don't worry.'

'If you'd like to give him a bash in the chops, sir,' said the top millicent, 'don't mind us. We'll hold him down. He must be another great disappointment to you.'

P. R. Deltoid then did something I never thought any man like him who was supposed to turn us baddiwads into real horrorshow malchicks would do, especially with all those rozzes around. He came a bit nearer and he spat. He spat. He spat full in my litso and then wiped his wet spitty rot with the back of his rooker. And I wiped and wiped and wiped my spat-on litso with my bloody tashtook, saying: 'Thank you, sir, thank you very much, sir, that was very kind of you, sir, thank you.' And then P. R. Deltoid walked out without another slovo.

The millicents now got down to making this long statement for me to sign, and I thought to myself, Hell and blast you all, if all you bastards are on the side of the Good then I'm glad I belong to the other shop. 'All right,' I said to them, 'you grahzny bratchnies as you are, you vonny sods. Take it, take the lot. I'm not going to crawl around on my brooko any more, you merzky gets. Where do you want it taking from, you cally vonning animals? From my last corrective?

Horrorshow, horrorshow, here it is, then.' So I gave it to them, and I had this shorthand millicent, a very quiet and scared type chelloveck, no real rozz at all, covering page after page after page after. I gave them the ultra-violence, the crasting, the dratsing, the old in-out-in-out, the lot, right up to this night's veshch with the bugatty starry ptitsa with the mewing kots and koshkas. And I made sure my so-called droogs were in it, right up to the shiyah. When I'd got through the lot the shorthand millicent looked a bit faint, poor old veck. The top rozz said to him, in a kind type goloss:

'Right, son, you go off and get a nice cup of chai for yourself and then type all that filth and rottenness out with a clothes-peg on your nose, three copies. Then they can be brought to our handsome young friend here for signature. And you,' he said to me, 'can now be shown to your bridal suite with running water and all conveniences. All right,' in this weary goloss to two of the real tough rozzes, 'take him away.'

So I was kicked and punched and bullied off to the cells and put in with about ten or twelve other plennies, a lot of them drunk. There were real oozhassny animal type vecks among them, one with his nose all ate away and his rot open like a big black hole, one that was lying on the floor snoring away and all like slime dribbling all the time out of his rot, and one that had like done all cal in his pantalonies. Then there were two like queer ones who both took a fancy to me, and one of them made a jump on to my back, and I had a real nasty bit of dratsing with him and the von on him, like of meth and cheap scent, made me want to sick again, only my belly was empty now, O my brothers. Then the other queer one started putting his rookers on to me, and then there was a snarling bit of dratsing between these two, both of them wanting to get at my plott. The shoom became very loud, so that a couple of millicents came along and cracked into these two with like truncheons, so that both sat quiet then, looking like into space, and there was the old krovvy going drip drip drip down the litso of one of them. There were bunks in this cell, but all filled. I climbed up to the top one of one tier of bunks, there being four in a tier, and there was a starry drunken veck snoring away, most probably heaved up there to the top by the millicents. Anyway, I heaved him down again, him not being all that heavy, and he collapsed on top of a fat drunk chelloveck on the floor, and both woke and started creeching and punching pathetic at each other. So I lay down on this vonny bed, my brothers, and went to very tired and exhausted and hurt sleep. But it was not really like sleep, it was like passing out to another better world. And in this other better world, O my brothers, I was in like a big field with all flowers and trees, and there was a like goat with a man's litso playing away on a like flute. And then there rose like the sun Ludwig van himself with thundery litso and cravat and wild windy voloss, and then I heard the Ninth, last movement, with the slovos all a bit mixed-up like they knew themselves they had to be mixed-up, this being a dream:

> Boy, thou uproarious shark of heaven,
>> Slaughter of Elysium,
> Hearts on fire, aroused, enraptured,
>> We will tolchock you on the rot and kick
>> your grahzny vonny bum.

But the tune was right, as I knew when I was being woke up two or ten minutes or twenty hours or days or years later, my watch having been taken away. There was a millicent like miles and miles down below and he was prodding at me with a long stick with a spike on the end, saying:

'Wake up, son. Wake up, my beauty. Wake to real trouble.' I said:

'Why? Who? Where? What is it?' And the tune of the Joy ode in the Ninth was singing away real lovely and horrorshow within. The millicent said:

'Come down and find out. There's some real lovely news for you, my son.' So I scrambled down, very stiff and sore and not like real awake, and this rozz, who had a strong von of cheese and onions on him, pushed me out of the filthy snoring cell, and then along corridors, and all the time the old tune Joy Thou Glorious Spark Of Heaven was sparking away within. Then we came to a very neat like cantora with typewriters and flowers on the desks, and at the like chief desk the top millicent was sitting, looking very serious and fixing a like very cold glazzy on my sleepy litso. I said:

'Well, well, well. What makes. bratty. What gives, this fine bright middle of the nochy?' He said:

'I'll give you just ten seconds to wipe that stupid grin off of your face. Then I want you to listen.'

'Well, what?' I said, smecking. 'Are you not satisfied with beating me near to death and having me spat upon and making me confess to crimes for hours on end and then shoving me among bezoomnies and vonny perverts in that grahzny cell? Have you some new torture for me, you bratchny?'

'It'll be your own torture,' he said, serious. I hope to God it'll torture you to madness.'

And then, before he told me, I knew what it was. The old ptitsa who had all the kots and koshkas had passed on to a better world in one of the city hospitals. I'd cracked her a bit too hard, like. Well, well, that was everything. I thought of all those kots and koshkas mewing for moloko and getting none, not any more from their starry forella of a mistress. That was everything. I'd done the lot, now. And me still only fifteen.

# Part Two

## 1

'What's it going to be then, eh?'

I take it up now, and this is the real weepy and like tragic part of the story beginning, my brothers and only friends, in Staja (State Jail, that is) Number 84F. You will have little desire to slooshy all the cally and horrible raskazz of the shock that sent my dad beating his bruised and krovvy rockers against unfair like Bog in his Heaven, and my mum squaring her rot for owwwww owwwww owwwww in her mother's grief at her only child and son of her bosom like letting everybody down real horrorshow. Then there was the starry very grim magistrate in the lower court govoreeting some very hard slovos against your Friend and Humble Narrator, after all the cally and grahzny slander spat forth by P. R. Deltoid and the rozzes, Bog blast them. Then there was being remanded in filthy custody among vonny perverts and prestoopnicks. Then there was the trial in the higher court with judges and a jury, and some very very nasty slovos indeed govoreeted in a very like solemn way, and then Guilty and my mum boohoohooing when they said Fourteen Years, O my brothers. So here I was now, two years just to the day of being kicked and clanged into Staja 84F, dressed in the heighth of prison fashion, which was a one-piece suit of a very filthy like cal colour, and the number sewn on the groody part just above the old tick-tocker and on the back as well, so that going and coming I was 6655321 and not your little droog Alex not no longer.

'What's it going to be then, eh?'

It had not been like edifying, indeed it had not, being in this grahzny

57

hellhole and like human zoo for two years, being kicked and tolchocked by brutal bully warders and meeting vonny leering like criminals, some of them real perverts and ready to dribble all over a luscious young malchick like your story-teller. And there was having to rabbit in the workshop at making matchboxes and itty round and round and round the yard for like exercise, and in the evenings sometimes some starry prof type veck would give a talk on beetles or the Milky Way or the Glorious Wonders of the Snowflake, and I had a good smeck at this last one, because it reminded me of that time of the tolchocking and Sheer Vandalism with that ded coming from the public biblio on a winter's night when my droogs were still not traitors and I was like happy and free. Of those droogs I had slooshied but one thing, and that was one day when my pee and em came to visit and I was told that Georgie was dead. Yes, dead, my brothers. Dead as a bit of dog-cal on the road. Georgie had led the other two into a like very rich chelloveck's house, and there they had kicked and tolchocked the owner on the floor, and then Georgie had started to razrez the cushions and curtains, and then old Dim had cracked at some very precious ornaments, like statues and so on, and this rich beat-up chelloveck had raged like real bezoomny and gone for them all with a very heavy iron bar. His being all razdraz had given him some gigantic strength, and Dim and Pete had got out through the window but Georgie had tripped on the carpet and then brought this terrific swinging iron bar crack and splooge on the gulliver, and that was the end of traitorous Georgie. The starry murderer had got off with Self Defence, as was really right and proper. Georgie being killed, though it was more than one year after me being caught by the millicents, it all seemed right and proper and like Fate.

'What's it going to be then, eh?'

I was in the Wing Chapel, it being Sunday morning, and the prison charlie was govoreeting the Word of the Lord. It was my rabbit to play the starry stereo, putting on solemn music before and after and in the middle too when hymns were sung. I was at the back of the Wing Chapel (there were four along here in Staja 84F) near where the warders or chassos were standing with their rifles and their dirty bolshy blue brutal jowls, and I could viddy all the plennies sitting down slooshying the Slovo of the Lord in their horrible cal-coloured prison platties, and a sort of filthy von rose from them, not like real unwashed, not grazzy, but like a special real stinking von which you only got with the criminal types, my brothers, a like dusty, greasy, hopeless sort of a von. And I was thinking that perhaps I had this von too, having become a real penny myself, though still very young. So it was very important to me, O my brothers, to get out of this stinking grahzny zoo as soon as I could. And, as you will viddy if you keep reading on, it was not long before I did.

'What's it going to be then, eh?' said the prison charlie for the third raz. 'Is it going to be in and out and in and out of institutions, like this, though more in than out for most of you, or are you going to attend to the Divine Word and realize the punishments that await the unrepentant sinner in the next world, as well as in this? A lot of blasted idiots you are, most of you, selling your birthright for a saucer of cold porridge. The thrill of theft, of violence, the urge to live easy – is it worth it when we have undeniable proof, yes yes, incontrovertible evidence that hell exists? I know, I know, my friends, I have been informed in visions that there is a place, darker than any prison, hotter than any flame of human fire, where souls of unrepentant criminal sinners like yourselves – and don't leer at me, damn you, don't laugh – like yourselves, I say, scream in endless and intolerable agony, their noses choked with the smell of filth, their mouths crammed with burning ordure, their skin peeling and rotting, a fireball spinning in their screaming guts. Yes, yes, yes, I know.'

At this point, brothers, a plenny somewhere or other near the back row let out a shoom of lip-music – 'Prrrrrp' – and then the brutal chassos were on the job right away, rushing real skorry to what they thought was the scene of the schoom, then hitting out nasty and delivering tolchocks left and right. Then they picked out one poor trembling plenny, very thin and malenky and starry too, and dragged him off, but all the time he kept creeching: 'It wasn't me, it was him, see,' but that made no difference. He was tolchocked real nasty and then dragged out of the Wing Chapel creeching his gulliver off.

'Now,' said the prison charlie, 'listen to the Word of the Lord.' Then he picked up the big book and flipped over the pages, keeping on wetting his fingers to do this by licking them splurge splurge. He was a bolshy great burly bastard with a very red litso, but he was very fond of myself, me being young and also now very interested in the big book. It had been arranged as part of my like further education to read in the book and even have music on the chapel stereo while I was reading. O my brothers. And that was real horrorshow. They would like lock me in and let me slooshy holy music by J. S. Bach and G. F. Handel, and I would read of these starry yahoodies tolchocking each other and then peeting their Hebrew vino and getting on to the bed with their wives' like hand-maidens, real horrorshow. That kept me going, brothers. I didn't so much kopat the later part of the book, which is more like all preachy govoreeting than fighting and the old in-out. But one day the charles said to me, squeezing me like tight with his bolshy beefy rooker: 'Ah, 6655321, think on the divine suffering. Meditate on that, my boy.' And all the time he had this rich manny von of Scotch on him, and then he went off to his little cantora to peet some more. So I read all about the scourging and the crowning with thorns and then the cross veshch and all that cal, and I viddied better that there was something in it. While the stereo played bits of lovely Bach I closed my glazzies and viddied myself helping in and even taking charge of the tolchocking and the nailing in, being dressed in a like toga that was the heighth of Roman fashion. So being in Staja 84F was not all that wasted, and the Governor himself was very pleased to hear that I had taken to like Religion, and that was where I had my hopes.

This Sunday morning the charlie read out from the book about chellovecks who slooshied the slovo and didn't take a blind bit being like a domy built upon sand, and then the rain came splash and the old boomaboom cracked the sky and that was the end of that domy. But I thought that only a very dim veck would build his domy upon sand, and a right lot of real sneering droogs and nasty neighbours a veck like that would have, them not telling him how dim he was doing that sort of building. Then the charles creeched: 'Right, you lot. We'll end with Hymn Number 435 in the Prisoners' Hymnal.' Then there was a crash and plop and a whish whish while the plennies picked up and dropped and lickturned the pages of their grazzy malenky hymnbooks, and the bully fierce warders creeched: 'Stop talking there, bastards. I'm watching you, 920537.' Of course I had the disc ready on the stereo, and then I let the simple music for organ only come belting out with a growwwwowwwwowwww. Then the plennies started to sing real horrible:

> Weak tea are we, new brewed
> But stirring make all strong.
> We eat no angel's food,
> Our times of trial are long.

They sort of howled and wept these stupid slovos with the charlie like whipping them on with 'Louder, damn you, sing up,' and the warders creeching: 'Just you wait, 7749222', and 'One on the turnip coming up for you, filth.' Then it was all over and the charlie said: 'May the Holy Trinity keep you always and make you good, amen,' and the shamble out began to a nice choice bit of Symphony No. 2 by Adrian Schweigselber, chosen by your Humble Narrator, O my brothers. What a lot they were, I thought, as I stood there by the starry chapel stereo, viddying them all shuffle out going marrrrre and baaaaaa like animals and up-your-piping with their grahzny fingers at me, because it looked like I was very special favoured. When the last one had slouched out, his rookers hanging like an ape and the one warder left giving him a fair loud tolchock on the back of the gulliver, and when I had turned off the stereo, the charlie came up to me, puffing away at a cancer, still in his starry bogman's platties, all lacy and white like a devotchka's. He said:

'Thank you as always, little 6655321. And what news have you got for me today?' The idea was, I knew, that this charlie was after becoming a very great holy chelloveck in the world of Prison Religion, and he wanted a real horrorshow testimonial from the Governor, so he would go and govoreet quietly to the Governor now and then about what dark plots were brewing among the plennies, and he would get a lot of this cal from me. A lot of it would be all like made up, but some of it would be true, like for instance the time it had come through to our cell on the waterpipes knock knock knockiknockiknock knockiknock that big Harriman was going to break. He was going to tolchock the warder at slop-time and get out in the warder's platties. Then there was going to be a big throwing about of the horrible pishcha we got in the dining-hall, and I knew about that and told. Then the charlie passed it on and was complimented like by the Governor for his Public Spirit and Keen Ear. So this time I said, and this was not true:

'Well, sir, it has come through on the pipes that a consignment of cocaine has arrived by irregular means and that a cell somewhere along Tier 5 is to be the centre of distribution.' I made all that up as I went along, like I made up so many of these stories, but the prison charlie was very grateful, saying: 'Good, good, good. I shall pass that on to Himself,' this being what he called the Governor. Then I said:

'Sir, I have done my best, have I not?' I always used my very polite gentleman's goloss govoreeting with those at the top. 'I've tried, sir, haven't I?'

'I think,' said the charlie, 'that on the whole you have, 6655321. You've been very helpful and, I consider, shown a genuine desire to reform. You will, if you continue in this manner, earn your remission with no trouble at all.'

'But sir,' I said, 'how about this new thing they're talking about? How about this new like treatment that gets you out of prison in no time at all and makes sure that you never get back in again?'

'Oh,' he said, very like wary. 'Where did you hear this? Who's been telling you these things?'

'These things get around, sir,' I said. 'Two warders talk, as it might be, and somebody can't help hearing what they say. And then somebody picks up a scrap of newspaper in the workshops and the newspaper says all about it. How about you putting me in for this thing, sir, if I may make so bold as to make the suggestion?'

You could viddy him thinking about that while he puffed away at his cancer, wondering how much to say to me about what he knew about this veshch I'd mentioned. Then he said: 'I take it you're referring to Ludovico's Technique.' He was still very wary.

'I don't know what it's called, sir,' I said. 'All I know is that it gets you out quickly and makes sure that you don't get in again.'

'That is so,' he said, his eyebrows like all beetling while he looked down at me. 'That is quite so, 6655321. Of course, it's only in the experimental stage at the moment. It's very simple but very drastic.'

'But it's being used here, isn't it, sir?' I said. 'Those new like white buildings by the South wall, sir. We've watched those being built, sir, when we've been doing our exercise.'

'It's not been used yet,' he said, 'not in this prison, 6655321. Himself has grave doubts about it. I must confess I share those doubts. The question is whether such a technique can really make a man good. Goodness comes from within, 6655321. Goodness is something chosen. When a man cannot choose he ceases to be a man.' He would have gone on with a lot more of this cal, but we could slooshy the next lot of plennies marching clank clank down the iron stairs to come for their bit of religion. He said: 'We'll have a little chat about this some other time. Now you'd better start the voluntary.' So I went over to the starry stereo and put on J. S. Bach's *Wachet Auf* Choral Prelude and in there the grahzny vonny bastard criminals and perverts came shambling like a lot of broke-down apes, the warders or chassos like barking at them and lashing them. And soon the prison charlie was asking them: 'What's it going to be then, eh?' And that's where you came in.

We had four of these lomticks of like Prison Religion that morning, but the charles said no more to me about this Ludovico's Technique, whatever it was, O my brothers. When I'd finished my rabbit with the stereo he just govoreeted a few slovos of thanks and then I was privodeeted back to the cell on Tier 6 which was my very vonny and crammed home. The chasso was not really too bad of a veck and he did not tolchock or kick me in when he'd opened up, he just said: 'Here we are, sonny, back to the old waterhole.' And there I was with my new type droogs, all very criminal but, Bog be praised, not given to perversions of the body. There was Zophar on his bunk, a very thin and brown veck who went on and on and on in his like cancery goloss, so that nobody bothered to slooshy. What he was saying now like to nobody was 'And at that time you couldn't get hold of a poggy' (whatever that was, brothers), 'not if you was to hand over ten million archibalds, so what do I do, eh, I goes down to Turkey's and says I've got this sproog on that morrow, see, and what can he do?' It was all this very old-time real criminal's slang he spoke. Also there was Wall, who had only one glazzy, and he was tearing bits of his toe-nails off in honour of Sunday. Also there was Big Jew, a very fast sweaty veck lying flat on his bunk like dead. In addition there was Jojohn and The Doctor. Jojohn was very mean and keen and wiry and had specialized in like Sexual Assault, and The Doctor had pretended to be able to cure syph and gon and gleet but he had only injected water, also he had killed off two devotchkas instead, like he had promised, of getting rid of their unwanted loads for them. They were a terrible grahzny lot really, and I didn't enjoy being with them, O my brothers, any more than you do now, but it won't be for much longer.

Now what I want you to know is that this cell was intended for only three when it was built, but there were six of us there, all jammed together sweaty and tight. And that was the state of all the cells in all the prisons in those days, brothers, and a dirty cally disgrace it was, there not being decent room for a chelloveck to stretch his limbs. And you will hardly believe what I say now, which is that on this Sunday they brosatted in another plenny. Yes, we had had our horrible pishcha of dumplings and vonny stew and were smoking a quiet cancer each on our bunks when this veck was thrown into our midst. He was a chinny starry veck and it was him who started creeching complaints before we even had a chance to viddy the position. He tried to like shake the bars, creeching: 'I demand my sodding rights, this one's full-up, it's a bleeding imposition, that's what it is.' But one of the chassos came back to say that he had to make the best of it and share a bunk with whoever would let him, otherwise it would have to be the floor. 'And,' said the warder, 'it's going to get worse, not better. A right dirty criminal world you lot are trying to build.'

2

Well, it was the letting-in of this new chelloveck that was really the start of my getting out of the old Staja, for he was such a nasty quarrelsome type of plenny, with a very dirty mind and filthy intentions, that trouble nachinatted that very same day. He was also very boastful and started to make with a very sneery litso at us all and a loud proud goloss. He made out that he was the only real horrorshow prestoopnick in the whole zoo, going on that he'd done this and done the other and killed ten rozzes with one crack of his rooker and all that cal. But nobody was very impressed, O my brothers. So then he started on me, me being the youngest there, trying to say that as the youngest I ought to be the one to zasnoot on the floor and not him. But all the others were for me, creeching: 'Leave him alone, you grahzny bratchny,' and then he began the old whine about how nobody loved him. So that same nochy I woke up to find this horrible plenny actually lying with me on my bunk, which was on the bottom of the three-tier and also very narrow, and he was govoreeting dirty like love-slovos and stroke stroke stroking away. So then I got real bezoomny and lashed out, though I could not viddy all that horrorshow, there being only this malenky little red light outside on the landing. But I knew it was this one, the vonny bastard, and then when the trouble really got under way and the lights were turned on I could viddy his horrible litso with all krovvy dripping from his rot where I'd hit out with my clawing rooker.

What sloochatted then, of course, was that my cell-mates woke up and started to join in, tolchocking a bit wild in the near-dark, and the shoom seemed to wake up the whole tier, so that you could slooshy a lot of creeching and banging about with tin mugs on the wall, as though all the plennies in all the cells thought a big break was about to commence, O my brothers. So then the lights came on and the chassos came along in their shirts and trousers and caps, waving big sticks. We could viddy each other's flushed litsos and the shaking of fisty rookers, and there was a lot of creeching and cursing. Then I put in my complaint and every chasso said it was probably Your Humble Narrator, brothers, that started it all anyway, me having no mark of a scratch on me but this horrible plenny dipping red red krovvy from the rot where I'd got him with my clawing rooker. That made me real bezoomny. I said I would not sleep another nochy in that cell if the Prison Authorities were going to allow horrible vonny stinking perverted prestoopnicks to leap on my plott when I was in no position to defend myself, being asleep. 'Wait till the morning,' they said. 'Is it a private room with bath and television that your honour requires? Well, all that will be seen to in the morning. But for the present, little droog, get your bleeding gulliver down on your straw-filled podooshka and let's have no more trouble from anyone. Right right right?' Then off they went with stern warnings for all, then soon after the lights went out, and then I said I would sit up all the rest of the nochy, saying first to this horrible prestoopnick: 'Go on, get on my bunk if you wish it. I fancy it no longer. You have made it filthy and cally with your horrible vonny plott lying on it already.' But then the others joined in. Big Jew said, still sweating from the bit of a bitva we'd had in the dark:

'Not having that we're not, brotherth. Don't give in to the thquirt.' So this new one said:

'Crash your dermott, yid,' meaning to shut up, but it was very insulting. So then Big Jew got ready to launch a tolchock. The Doctor said:

'Come on, gentlemen, we don't want any trouble, do we?' in his very high-class goloss, but this new prestoopnick was really asking for it. You could viddy that he thought he was a very big bolshy veck and it was beneath his dignity to be sharing a cell with six and having to sleep on the floor till I made this gesture at him. In his sneery way he tried to take off The Doctor, saying:

'Owwww, yew wahnt noo moor trouble, is that it, Archiballs?' So Jojohn, mean and keen and wiry, said:

'If we can't have sleep let's have some education. Our new friend here had better be taught a lesson.' Although he like specialized in Sexual Assault he had a nice way of govoreeting, quiet and like precise. So the new plenny sneered:

'Kish and kosh and koosh, you little terror.' So then it all really started, but in a queer like gentle way, with nobody raising his goloss much. The new plenny creeched a malenky bit at first, but the Wall fisted his rot while Big Jew held him up against the bars so that he could be viddied in the malenky red light from the landing, and he just went oh oh oh. He was not a very strong type of veck, being very feeble in his trying to tolchock back, and I suppose he made up for this by being shoomny in the goloss and very boastful. Anyway, seeing the old krovvy flow red in the red light, I felt the old joy like rising up in my keeshkas and I said:

'Leave him to me, go on, let me have him now, brothers.' So Big Jew said:

'Yeth, yeth, boyth, that'th fair. Thlosh him then, Alekth.' So they all stood around while I cracked at this prestoopnick in the near dark. I fisted him all over, dancing about with my boots on though unlaced, and then I tripped him and he went crash crash on to the floor. I gave him one real horrorshow kick on the gulliver and he went ohhhhh, then he sort of snorted off to like sleep, and The Doctor said:

'Very well, I think that will be enough of a lesson,' squinting to viddy this downed and beaten-up veck on the floor. 'Let him dream perhaps about being a better boy in the future.' So we all climbed back into our bunks, being very tired now. What I dreamt of, O my brothers, was of being in some very big orchestra, hundreds and hundreds strong, and the conductor was a like mixture of Ludwig van and G. F. Handel, looking very deaf and blind and weary of the world. I was with the wind instruments, but what I was playing was like a white pinky bassoon made of flesh and growing out of my plott, right in the middle of my belly, and when I blew into it I had to smeck ha ha ha very loud because it like tickled, and then Ludwig van G. F. got very razdraz and bezoomny. Then he came right up to my litso and creeched loud in my ooko, and then I woke up like sweating. Of course, what the loud shoom really was was the prison buzzer going brrrrr brrrrr brrrrr. It was winter morning and my glazzies were all cally with sleepglue, and when I opened up they were very sore in the electric light that had been switched on all over the zoo. Then I looked down and viddied this new prestoopnick lying on the floor, very bloody and bruisy and still out out out. Then I remembered about last night and that made me smeck a bit.

But when I got off the bunk and moved him with my bare noga, there was a feel of like stiff coldness, so I went over to The Doctor's bunk and shook him, him always being very slow at waking up in the morning. But he was off his bunk skorry enough this time, and so were the others, except for Wall who slept like dead meat. 'Very unfortunate,' The Doctor said. 'A heart attack, that's what it must have been.' Then he said, looking round at us all: 'You really shouldn't have gone for him like that. It was most ill-advised really.' Jojohn said:

'Come come, doc, you weren't all that backward yourself in giving him a sly bit of fist.' Then Big Jew turned on me, saying:

'Alekth, you were too impetuouth. That latht kick wath a very very nathty one.' I began to get razdraz about this and said:

'Who started it, eh? I only got in at the end, didn't I?' I pointed at Jojohn and said: 'It was your idea.' Wall snored a bit loud, so I said: 'Wake that vonny bratchny up. It was him that kept on at his rot while Big Jew here had him up against the bars.' The Doctor said:

'Nobody will deny having a little hit at the man, to teach him a lesson so to speak, but it's apparent that you, my dear boy, with the forcefulness and, shall I say, heedlessness of youth, dealt him the coo de gras. It's a great pity.'

'Traitors,' I said. 'Traitors and liars,' because I could viddy it was all like before, two years before, when my so-called droogs had left me to the brutal rookers of the millicents. There was no trust anywhere in the world, O my brothers, the way I could see it. And Jojohn went and woke up Wall, and Wall was only too ready to swear that it was Your Humble Narrator that had done the real dirty tolchocking and brutality. When the chassos came along, and then the Chief Chasso, and then the Governor himself, all these cell-droogs of mine were very shoomny with tales of what I'd done to oobivat this worthless pervert whose krovvy-covered plott lay sacklike on the floor.

That was a very queer day, O my brothers. The dead plott was carried off, and then everybody in the whole prison had to stay locked up till further orders, and there was no pishcha given out, not even a mug of hot chai. We just all sat there, and the warders or chassos sort of strode up and down the tier, now and then creeching 'Shut it' or 'Close that hole' whenever they slooshied even a whisper from any of the cells. Then about eleven o'clock in the morning there was a sort of like stiffening and excitement and like the von of fear spreading from outside the cell, and then we could viddy the Governor and the Chief Chasso and some very bolshy important-looking chellovecks walking by real skorry, govoreeting like bezoomny. They seemed to walk right to the end of the tier, then they could be slooshied walking back again, more slow this time, and you could slooshy the Governor, a very sweaty fatty fair-haired veck, saying slovos like 'But, sir – ' and 'Well, what can be done, sir?' and so on. Then the whole lot stopped at our cell and the Chief Chasso opened up. You could viddy who was the real important veck right away, very tall and with blue glazzies and with real horrorshow platties on him, the most lovely suit, brothers, I had ever viddied, absolutely in the heighth of fashion. He just sort of looked right through us poor plennies, saying, in a very beautiful real educated goloss: 'The Government cannot be concerned any longer with outmoded penological theories. Cram criminals together and see what happens. You get concentrated criminality, crime in the midst of punishment. Soon we may be needing all our prison space for political offenders.' I didn't pony this at all, brothers, but after all he was not govoreeting to me. Then he said: 'Common criminals like this unsavoury crowd' – (that meant me, brothers, as well as the others, who were real prestoopnicks and treacherous with it) – 'can best be dealt with on a purely curative basis. Kill the criminal reflex, that's all. Full implementation in a year's time. Punishment means nothing to them, you can see that. They enjoy their so-called punishment. They start murdering each other.' And he turned his stern blue glazzies on me. So I said, bold:

'With respect, sir, I object very strongly to what you said then. I am not a common criminal, sir, and I am not unsavoury. The others may be unsavoury but I am not.' The Chief Chasso went all purple and creeched:

'You shut your bleeding hole, you. Don't you know who this is?'

'All right, all right,' said this big veck. Then he turned to the Governor and said: 'You can use him as a trail-blazer. He's young, bold, vicious. Brodsky will deal with him tomorrow and you can sit in and watch Brodsky. It works all right, don't worry about that. This vicious young hoodlum will be transformed out of all recognition.'

And those hard slovos, brothers, were like the beginning of my freedom.

# 3

That very same evening I was dragged down nice and gentle by brutal tolchocking chassos to viddy the Governor in his holy of holies holy office. The Governor looked very weary at me and said: 'I don't suppose you know who that was this morning, do you, 6655321?' And without waiting for me to say no he said: 'That was no less a personage than the Minister of the Interior, the new Minister of the Interior and what they call a very new broom. Well, these new ridiculous ideas have come at last and orders are orders, though I may say to you in confidence that I do not approve. I most emphatically do not approve. An eye for an eye, I say. If someone hits you you hit back, do you not? Why then should not the State, very severely hit by you brutal hooligans, not hit back also? But the new view is to say no. The new view is that we turn the bad into the good. All of which seems to me grossly unjust. Hm?' So I said, trying to be like respectful and accommodating:

'Sir.' And then the Chief Chasso, who was standing all red and burly behind the Governor's chair, creeched:

'Shut your filthy hole, you scum.'

'All right, all right,' said the like tired and fagged-out Governor. 'You, 6655321, are to be reformed. Tomorrow you go to this man Brodsky. It is believed that you will be able to leave State Custody in a little over a fortnight. In a little over a fortnight you will be out again in the big free world, no longer a number. I suppose,' and he snorted a bit here, 'that prospect pleases you?' I said nothing so the Chief Chasso creeched:

'Answer, you filthy young swine, when the Governor asks you a question.' So I said:

'Oh, yes, sir. Thank you very much, sir. I've done my best here, really I have. I'm very grateful to all concerned.'

'Don't be,' like sighed the Governor. 'This is not a reward. This is far from being a reward. Now, there is a form here to be signed. It says that you are willing to have the residue of your sentence commuted to submission to what is called here, ridiculous expression, Reclamation Treatment. Will you sign?'

'Most certainly I will sign,' I said, 'sir. And very many thanks.' So I was given an ink-pencil and I signed my name nice and flowy. The Governor said:

'Right. That's the lot, I think.' The Chief Chasso said:

'The Prison Chaplain would like a word with him, sir.' So I was marched out and off down the corridor towards the Wing Chapel, tolchocked on the back and the gulliver all the way by one of the chassos, but in a very like yawny and bored manner. And I was marched across the Wing Chapel to the little cantora of the charles and then made to go in. The charles was sitting at his desk, smelling loud and clear of a fine manny von of expensive cancers and Scotch. He said:

'Ah, little 6655321, be seated.' And to the chassos: 'Wait outside, eh?' Which they did. Then he spoke in a very like earnest way to me, saying: 'One thing I want you to understand, boy, is that this is nothing to do with me. Were it expedient, I would protest about it, but it is not expedient. There is the question of my own career, there is the question of the weakness of my own voice when set against the shout of certain more powerful elements in the polity. Do I make myself clear?' He didn't, brothers, but I nodded that he did. 'Very hard ethical questions are involved,' he went on. 'You are to be made into a good boy, 6655321. Never again will you have the desire to commit acts of violence or to offend in any way whatsoever against the State's Peace. I hope you take all that in. I hope you are absolutely clear in your own mind about that.' I said:

'Oh, it will be nice to be good, sir.' But I had a real horrorshow smeck at that inside, brothers. He said:

'It may not be nice to be good, little 6655321. It may be horrible to be good. And when I say that to you I realize how self-contradictory that sounds. I know I shall have many sleepless nights about this. What does God want? Does God want woodness or the choice of goodness? Is a man who chooses the bad perhaps in some way better than a man who has the good imposed upon him? Deep and hard questions, little 6655321. But all I want to say to you now is this: if at any time in the future you look back to these times and remember me, the lowest and humblest of all God's servitors, do not, I pray, think evil of me in your heart, thinking me in any way involved in what is now about to happen to you. And now, talking of praying, I realize sadly that there will be little point in praying for you. You are passing now to a region where you will be beyond the reach of the power of prayer. A terrible terrible thing to consider. And yet, in a sense, in choosing to be deprived of the ability to make an ethical choice, you have in a sense really chosen the good. So I shall like to think. So, God help us all, 6655321, I shall like to think.' And then he began to cry. But I didn't really take much notice of that, brothers only having a bit of a quiet smeck inside, because you could viddy that he had been peeting away at the old whisky, and now he took a bottle from a cupboard in his desk and started to pour himself a real horrorshow bolshy slog into a very greasy and grahzny glass. He downed it and then said: 'All may be well, who knows? God works in a mysterious way.' Then he began to sing away at a hymn in a real loud rich goloss. Then the door opened and the chassos came in to tolchock me back to my vonny cell, but the old charles still went on singing this hymn.

Well, the next morning I had to say good-bye to the old Staja, and I felt a malenky bit sad as you always will when you have to leave a place you've like got used to. But I didn't go very far, O my brothers. I was punched and kicked along to the new white building just beyond the yard where we used to do our bit of exercise. This was a very new building and it had a new cold like sizy smell which gave you a bit of the shivers. I stood there in the horrible bolshy bare hall and I got new vons, sniffing away there with my like very sensitive morder or sniffer. These were like hospital vons, and the chelloveck the chassos handed me over to had a white coat on, as he might be a hospital man. He signed for me, and one of the brutal chassos who had brought me said: 'You watch this one, sir. A right brutal bastard he has been and will be again, in spite of all his sucking up to the Prison Chaplain and reading the Bible.' But this new chelloveck had real horrorshow blue glazzies which like smiled when he govoreeted. He said:

'Oh, we don't anticipate any trouble. We're going to be friends, aren't we?' And he smiled with his glazzies and his fine big rot which was full of shining white zoobies and I sort of took to this veck right away. Anyway, he passed me on to a like lesser veck in a white coat, and this one was very nice too, and I was led off to a very nice white clean bedroom with curtains and a bedside lamp, and just the one bed in it, all for Your Humble Narrator. So I had a real horrorshow inner smeck at that, thinking I was really a very lucky young malchickiwick. I was told to take off my horrible prison platties and I was given a really beautiful set of pyjamas, O my brothers, in plain green, the heighth of bedwear fashion. And I was given a nice warm dressing-gown too and lovely toofles to put my bare nogas in, and I thought: 'Well, Alex boy, little 6655321 as was, you have copped it lucky and no mistake. You are really going to enjoy it here.'

After I had been given a nice chasha of real horrorshow coffee and some old gazettas and mags to look at while peeting it, this first veck in white came in, the one who had like signed for me, and he said: 'Aha, there you are,' a silly sort of a veshch to say but it didn't sound silly, this veck being so like nice. 'My name,' he said, 'is Dr Branom. I'm Dr Brodsky's assistant. With your permission, I'll just give you the usual brief overall examination.' And he took the old stetho out of his right carman. 'We must make sure you're quite fit, mustn't we? Yes indeed, we must.' So while I lay there with my pyjama top off and he did this, that and the other, I said:

'What exactly is it, sir, that you're going to do?'

'Oh,' said Dr Branom, his cold stetho going all down my back, 'it's quite simple, really. We just show you some films.'

'Films?' I said. I could hardly believe my ookos, brothers, as you may well understand. 'You mean,' I said, 'it will be just like going to the pictures?'

'They'll be special films,' said this Dr Branom. 'Very special films. You'll be having the first session this afternoon. Yes,' he said, getting up from bending over me, 'you seem to be quite a fit young boy. A bit under-nourished perhaps. That will be the fault of the prison food. Put your pyjama top back on. After every meal,' he said, sitting on the edge of the bed, 'we shall be giving you a shot in the arm. That should help.' I felt really grateful to this very nice Dr Branom. I said:

'Vitamins, sir, will it be?'

'Something like that,' he said, smiling real horrorshow and friendly.

'Just a jab in the arm after every meal.' Then he went out. I lay on the bed thinking this was like real heaven, and I read some of the mags they'd given me – *Worldsport, Sinny* (this being a film mag) and *Goal*. Then I lay back on the bed and shut my glazzies and thought how nice it was going to be out there again, Alex with perhaps a nice easy job during the day, me being now too old for the old skolliwoll, and then perhaps getting a new like gang together for the nochy, and the first rabbit would be to get old Dim and Pete, if they had not been got already by the millicents. This time I would be very careful not to get loveted. They were giving another like chance, me having done murder and all, and it would not be like fair to get loveted again, after going to all this trouble to show me films that were going to make me a real good malchick. I had a real horrorshow smeck at everybody's like innocence, and I was smecking my gulliver off when they brought in my lunch on a tray. The veck who brought it was the one who'd led me to this malenky bedroom when I came into the mesto, and he said:

'It's nice to know somebody's happy.' It was really a very nice appetizing bit of pishcha they'd laid out on the tray – two or three lomticks of like hot roastbeef with mashed kartoffel and vedge, then there was also ice-cream and a nice hot chasha of chai. And there was even a cancer to smoke and a matchbox with one match in. So this looked like it was the life, O my brothers. Then, about half an hour after while I was lying a bit sleepy on the bed, a woman nurse came in, a real nice young devotchka with real horrorshow groodies (I had not seen such for two years) and she had a tray and a hypodermic. I said:

'Ah, the old vitamins, eh?' And I clickclicked at her but she took no notice. All she did was to slam the needle into my left arm, and then swishhhh in went the vitamin stuff. Then she went out again, clack clack on her high-heeled nogas. Then the white-coated veck who was like a male nurse came in with a wheelchair. I was a malenky bit surprised to viddy that. I said:

'What giveth then, brother? I can walk, surely, to wherever we have to itty to.' But he said:

'Best I push you there.' And indeed, O my brothers, when I got off the bed I found myself a malenky bit weak. It was the under-nourishment like Dr Branom had said, all that horrible prison pishcha. But the vitamins in the after-meal injection would put me right. No doubt at all about that, I thought.

4

Where I was wheeled to, brothers, was like no sinny I had ever viddied before. True enough, one wall was all covered with silver screen, and direct opposite was a wall with square holes in for the projector to project through, and there were stereo speakers stuck all over the mesto. But against the right-hand one of the other walls was a bank of all like little meters, and in the middle of the floor facing the screen was like a dentist's chair with all lengths of wire running from it, and I had to like crawl from the wheelchair to this, being given some help by another like male nurse veck in a white coat. Then I noticed that underneath the projection holes was like all frosted glass and I thought I viddied shadows of like people moving behind it and I thought I slooshied somebody cough kashl kashl kashl. But then all I could like notice was how weak I seemed to be, and I put that down to changing over from prison pishcha to this new rich pishcha and the vitamins injected into me. 'Right,' said the wheelchair-wheeling veck, 'now I'll leave you. The show will commence as soon as Dr Brodsky arrives. Hope you enjoy it.' To be truthful, brothers, I did not really feel that I wanted to viddy any film-show this afternoon. I was just not in the mood. I would have liked much better to have a nice quiet spatchka on the bed, nice and quiet and all on my oddy knocky. I felt very limp.

What happened now was that one white-coated veck strapped my gulliver to a like head-rest, singing to himself all the time some vonny cally pop-song. 'What's this for?' I said. And this veck replied, interrupting his like song an instant, that it was to keep my gulliver still and make me look at the screen. 'But,' I said, 'I *want* to look at the screen. I've been brought here to viddy films and viddy films I shall.' And then the other white-coat veck (there were three altogether, one of them a devotchka who was like sitting at the bank of meters and twiddling with knobs) had a bit of a smeck at that. He said:

'You never know. Oh, you never know. Trust us, friend. It's better this way.' And then I found they were strapping my rookers to the chair-arms and my nogas were like stuck to a foot-rest. It seemed a bit bezoomny to me but I let them get on with what they wanted to get on with. If I was to be a free young malchick again in a fortnight's time I would put up with much in the meantime, O my brothers. One veshch I did not like, though, was when they put like clips on the skin of my forehead, so that my top glazz-lids were pulled up and up and up and I could not shut my glazzies no matter how I tried. I tried to smeck and said: 'This must be a real horrorshow film if you're so keen on my viddying it.' And one of the white-coat vecks said, smecking:

'Horrorshow is right, friend. A real show of horrors.' And then I had like a cap stuck on my gulliver and I could viddy all wires running away from it, and they stuck a like suction pad on my belly and one on the old tick-tocker, and I could just about viddy wires running away from those. Then there was the shoom of a door opening and you could tell some very important chelloveck was coming in by the way the white-coated under-vecks went all stiff. And then I viddied this Dr Brodsky. He was a malenky veck, very fat, with all curly hair curling all over his gulliver, and on his spuddy nose he had very thick ochkies. I could just viddy that he had a real horrorshow suit on, absolutely the heighth of fashion, and he had a like very delicate and subtle von of operating-theatres coming from him. With him was Dr Branom, all smiling like as though to give me confidence. 'Everything ready?' said Dr Brodsky in a very breathy goloss. Then I could slooshy voices saying Right right right from like a distance, then nearer to, then there was a quiet like humming shoom as though things had been switched on. And then the lights went out and there was Your Humble Narrator And Friend sitting alone in the dark, all on his frightened oddy knocky, not able to move nor shut his glazzies nor anything. And then, O my brothers, the film-show started off with some very gromky atmosphere music coming from the speakers, very fierce and full of discord. And then on the screen the picture came on, but there was no title and no credits. What came on was a street, as it might have been any street in any town, and it was a real dark nochy and the lamps were lit. It was a very good like professional piece of sinny, and there were none of these flickers and blobs you get, say, when you viddy one of these dirty films in somebody's house in a back street. All the time the music bumped out, very like sinister. And then you could viddy an old man coming down the street, very starry, and then there leaped out on this starry veck two malchicks dressed in the heighth of fashion, as it was at this time (still thin trousers but no like cravat any more, more of a real tie), and then they started to filly with him. You could slooshy his screams and moans, very realistic, and you could even get the like heavy breathing and panting of the two tolchocking malchicks. They made a real pudding out of this starry veck, going crack crack crack at him with the fisty rookers, tearing his platties off and then finishing up by booting his nagoy plott (this lay all krovvy-red in the grahzny mud of the gutter) and then running off very skorry. Then there was the close-up gulliver of this beaten-up starry veck, and the krovvy flowed beautiful red. It's funny how the colours of the like real world only seem really real when you viddy them on the screen.

Now all the time I was watching this I was beginning to get very aware of a like not feeling all that well, and this I put down to the under-nourishment and my stomach not quite ready for the rich pishcha and vitamins I was getting here. But I tried to forget this, concentrating on the next film which came on at once, my brothers, without any break at all. This time the film jumped right away on a young devotchka who was being given the old in-out by first one malchick then another then another then another, she creeching away very gromky through the speakers and like very pathetic and tragic music going on at the same time. This was real, very real, though if you thought about it properly you couldn't imagine lewdies actually agreeing to having all this done to them in a film, and if these films were made by the Good or the State you couldn't imagine them being allowed to take these films without like interfering with what was going on. So it must have been very clever what they call cutting or editing or some such veshch. For it was very real. And when it came to the sixth or seventh malchick leering and smecking and then going into it and the devotchka creeching on the sound-track like bezoomny, then I began to feel sick. I had like pains all over and felt I could sick up and at the same time not sick up, and I began to feel like in distress, O my brothers, being fixed rigid too on this chair. When this bit of film was over I could slooshy the goloss of this Dr Brodsky from over by the switchboard saying: 'Reaction about twelve point five? Promising, promising.'

Then we shot straight into another lomtick of film, and this time it was of just a human litso, a very like pale human face held still and having different nasty veshches done to it. I was sweating a malenky bit with the pain in my guts and a horrible thirst and my gulliver going throb throb throb, and it seemed to me that if I could not viddy this bit of film I would perhaps be not so sick. But I could not shut my glazzies, and even if I tried to move my glazz-balls about I still could not get like out of the line of fire of this picture. So I had to go on viddying what was being done and hearing the most ghastly creechings coming from this litso. I knew it could not really be *real*, but that made no difference. I was heaving away but could not sick, viddying first a britva cut out an eye, then slice down the cheek, then go rip rip rip all over, while red krovvy shot on to the camera lens. Then all the teeth were like wrenched out with a pair of pliers, and the creeching and the blood were terrific. Then I slooshied this very pleased goloss of Dr Brodsky going: 'Excellent, excellent, excellent.'

The next lomtick of film was of an old woman who kept a shop being kicked about amid very gromky laughter by a lot of malchicks, and these malchicks broke up the shop and then set fire to it. You could viddy this poor starry ptitsa trying to crawl out of the flames, screaming and creeching, but having had her leg broke by these malchicks kicking her she could not move. So then all the flames went roaring round her, and you could viddy her agonized litso like appealing through the flames and then disappearing in the flames, and then you could slooshy the most gromky and agonized and agonizing screams that ever came from a human goloss. So this time I knew I had to sick up, so I creeched:

'I want to be sick. Please let me be sick. Please bring something for me to be sick into.' But this Dr Brodsky called back:

'Imagination only. You've nothing to worry about. Next film coming up.' That was perhaps meant to be a joke, for I heard a like smeck coming from the dark. And then I was forced to viddy a most nasty film about Japanese torture. It was the 1939–45 War, and there were soldiers being fixed to trees with nails and having fires lit under them and having their yarbles cut off, and you even viddied a gulliver being sliced off a soldier with a sword, and then with his head rolling about and the rot and glazzies looking alive still, the plott of this soldier actually ran about, krovvying like a fountain out of the neck, and then it dropped, and all the time there was very very loud laughter from the Japanese. The pains I felt now in my belly and the headache and the thirst were terrible, and they all seemed to be coming out of the screen. So I creeched:

'Stop the film! Please, please stop it! I can't stand any more.' And then the goloss of this Dr Brodsky said:

'Stop it? *Stop it*, did you say? Why, we've hardly started.' And he and the others smecked quite loud.

## 5

I do not wish to describe, brothers, what other horrible veshches I was like forced to viddy that afternoon. The like minds of this Dr Brodsky and Dr Branom and the others in white coats, and remember there was this devotchka twiddling with the knobs and watching the meters, they must have been more cally and filthy than any prestoopnick in the Staja itself. Because I did not think it was possible for any veck to even think of making films of what I was forced to viddy, all tied to this chair and my glazzies made to be wide open. All I could do was to creech very gromky for them to turn it off, turn it off, and that like part drowned the noise of dratsing and fillying and also the music that went with it all. You can imagine it was like a terrible relief when I'd viddied the last bit of film, and this Dr Brodsky said, in a very yawny and bored like goloss: 'I think that should be enough for Day One, don't you, Branom?' And there I was with the lights switched on, my gulliver throbbing like a bolshy big engine that makes pain, and my rot all dry and cally inside, and feeling I could like sick up every bit of pishcha I had ever eaten, O my brothers, since the day I was like weaned. 'All right,' said this Dr Brodsky, 'he can be taken back to his bed.' Then he like patted me on the pletcho and said: 'Good, good. A very promising start,' grinning all over his litso, then he like waddled out, Dr Branom after him, but Dr Branom gave me a like very droogy and sympathetic type smile as though he had nothing to do with all this veshch but was like forced into it as I was.

Anyhow, they freed my plott from the chair and they let go the skin above my glazzies so that I could open and shut them again, and I shut them, O my brothers, with the pain and throb in my gulliver, and then I was like carried to the old wheelchair and taken back to my malenky bedroom, the under-veck who wheeled me singing away at some hound-and-horny popsong so that I like snarled: 'Shut it, thou,' but he only smecked and said: 'Never mind, friend,' and then sang louder. So I was put into the bed and still felt bolnoy but could not sleep, but soon I started to feel that soon I might start to feel that I might soon start feeling just a malenky bit better, and then I was brought some nice hot chai with plenty of moloko and sakar and, peeting that, I knew that that like horrible nightmare was in the past and all over. And then Dr Branom came in, all nice and smiling. He said:

'Well, by my calculations you should be starting to feel all right again. Yes?'

'Sir,' I said, like wary. I did not quite kopat what he was getting at govoreeting about calculations, seeing that getting better from feeling bolnoy is like your own affair and nothing to do with calculations. He sat down, all nice and droogy, on the bed's edge and said:

'Dr Brodsky is pleased with you. You had a very positive response. Tomorrow, of course, there'll be two sessions, morning and afternoon, and I should imagine that you'll be feeling a bit limp at the end of the day. But we have to be hard on you, you have to be cured.' I said:

'You mean I have to sit through –? You mean I have to look at –? Oh, no,' I said. 'It was horrible.'

'Of course it was horrible,' smiled Dr Branom. 'Violence is a very horrible thing. That's what you're learning now. Your body is learning it.'

'But,' I said, 'I don't understand. I don't understand about feeling sick like I did. I never used to feel sick before. I used to feel like very the opposite. I mean, doing it or watching it I used to feel real horrorshow. I just don't understand why or how or what –'

'Life is a very wonderful thing,' said Dr Branom in a like very holy goloss. 'The processes of life, the make-up of the human organism, who can fully understand these miracles? Dr Brodsky is, of course, a remarkable man. What is happening to you now is what should happen to any normal healthy human organism contemplating the actions of the forces of evil, the workings of the principle of destruction. You are being made sane, you are being made healthy.'

'That I will not have,' I said, 'nor can understand at all. What you've been doing is to make me feel very very ill.'

'Do you feel ill now?' he said, still with the old droogy smile on his litso. 'Drinking tea, resting, having a quiet chat with a friend – surely you're not feeling anything but well?'

I like listened and felt for pain and sickness in my gulliver and plott, in a like cautious way, but it was true, brothers, that I felt real horrorshow and even wanting my dinner. 'I don't get it,' I said. 'You must be doing something to me to make me feel ill.' And I sort of frowned about that, thinking.

'You felt ill this afternoon,' he said, 'because you're getting better. When we're healthy we respond to the presence of the hateful with fear and nausea. You're becoming healthy, that's all. You'll be healthier still this time tomorrow.' Then he patted me on the noga and went out, and I tried to puzzle the whole veshch out as best I could. What it seemed to me was that the wire and other veshches that were fixed to my plott perhaps were making me feel ill, and that it was all a trick really. I was still puzzling out all this and wondering whether I should refuse to be strapped down to this chair tomorrow and start a real bit of dratsing with them all, because I had my rights, when another chelloveck came in to see me. He was a like smiling starry veck who said he was what he called the Discharge Officer, and he carried a lot of bits of paper with him. He said:

'Where will you go when you leave here?' I hadn't really thought about that sort of veshch at all, and it only now really began to dawn on me that I'd be a fine free malchick very soon, and then I viddied that would only be if I played it everybody's way and did not start any dratsing and creeching and refusing and so on. I said:

'Oh, I shall go home. Back to my pee and em.'

'Your –?' He didn't get nadsat-talk at all, so I said:

'To my parents in the dear old flatblock.'

'I see,' he said. 'And when did you last have a visit from your parents?'

'A month,' I said, 'very near. They like suspended visiting-day for a bit because of one prestoopnick getting some blasting-powder smuggled in across the wires from his ptitsa. A real cally trick to play on the innocent, like punishing them as well. So it's near a month since I had a visit.'

'I see,' said this veck. 'And have your parents been informed of your transfer and impending release?' That had a real lovely zvook that did, that slovo *release*. I said:

'No.' Then I said: 'It will be a nice surprise for them, that, won't it? Me just walking in through the door and saying: "Here I am, back, a free veck again." Yes, real horrorshow.'

'Right,' said the Discharge Officer veck, 'we'll leave it at that. So long as you have somewhere to live. Now, there's the question of your having a job, isn't there?' And he showed me this long list of jobs I could have, but I thought, well, there would be time enough for that. A nice malenky holiday first. I could do a crasting job soon as I got out and fill the old carmans with pretty polly, but I would have to be very careful and I would have to do the job all on my oddy knocky. I did not trust so-called droogs any more. So I told this veck to leave it a bit and we would govoreet about it again. He said right right right, then got ready to leave. He showed himself to be a very queer sort of a veck, because what he did now was to like giggle and then say: 'Would you like to punch me in the face before I go?' I did not think I could possibly have slooshied that right, so I said:

'Eh?'

'Would you,' he giggled, 'like to punch me in the face before I go?' I frowned like at that, very puzzled, and said:

'Why?'

'Oh,' he said, 'just to see how you're getting on.' And he brought his litso real near, a fat grin all over his rot. So I fisted up and went smack at this litso, but he pulled himself away real skorry, grinning still, and my rooker just punched air. Very puzzling, this was, and I frowned as he left, smecking his gulliver off. And then, my brothers, I felt real sick again, just like in the afternoon, just for a couple of minootas. It then passed off skorry, and when they brought my dinner in I found I had a fair appetite and was ready to crunk away at the roast chicken. But it was funny that starry chelloveck asking for a tolchock in the litso. And it was funny feeling sick like that.

What was even funnier was when I went to sleep that night, O my brothers. I had a nightmare, and, as you might expect, it was of one of those bits of film I'd viddied in the afternoon. A dream or nightmare is really only like a film inside your gulliver, except that it is as though you could walk into it and be part of it. And this is what happened to me. It was a nightmare of one of the bits of film they showed me near the end of the afternoon like session, all of smecking malchicks doing the ultra-violent on a young ptitsa who was creeching away in her red red krovvy, her platties all razrezzed real horrorshow. I was in this fillying about, smecking away and being like the ring-leader, dressed in the heighth of nadsat fashion. And then at the heighth of all this dratsing and tolchocking I felt like paralysed and wanting to be very sick, and all the other malchicks had a real gromky smeck at me. Then I was dratsing my way back to being awake all through my own krovvy, pints and quarts and gallons of it, and then I found myself in my bed in this room. I wanted to be sick, so I got out of the bed all trembly so as to go off down the corridor to the old vaysay. But, behold, brothers, the door was locked. And turning round I viddied for like the first raz that there were bars on the window. And so, as I reached for the like pot in the malenky cupboard beside the bed, I viddied that there would be no escaping from any of all this. Worse, I did not dare to go back into my own sleeping gulliver. I soon found I did not want to be sick after all, but then I was poogly of getting back into bed to sleep. But soon I fell smack into sleep and did not dream any more.

## 6

'Stop it, stop it, stop it,' I kept on creeching out. 'Turn it off you grahzny bastards, for I can stand no more.' It was the next day, brothers, and I had truly done my best morning and afternoon to play it their way and sit like a horrorshow smiling cooperative malchick in the chair of torture while they flashed nasty bits of ultra-violence on the screen, my glazzies clipped open to viddy all, my plott and rookers and nogas fixed to the chair so I could not get away. What I was being made to viddy now was not really a veshch I would have thought to be too bad before, it being only three or four malchicks crasting in a shop and filling their carmans with cutter, at the same time fillying about with the creeching starry ptitsa running the shop, tolchoking her and letting the red red krovvy flow. But the throb and like crash crash crash in my gulliver and the wanting to be sick and the terrible dry rasping thirstiness in my rot, all were worse than yesterday. 'Oh, I've had enough' I cried. 'It's not fair, you vonny sods,' and I tried to struggle out of the chair but it was not possible, me being as good as stuck to it.

'First-class,' creeched out this Dr Brodsky. 'You're doing really well. Just one more and then we're finished.'

What it was now was the starry 1939—45 War again, and it was a very blobby and liny and crackly film you could viddy had been made by the Germans. It opened with German eagles and the Nazi flag with that like crooked cross that all malchicks at school love to draw, and then there were very haughty and nadmenny like German officers walking through streets that were all dust and bomb-holes and broken buildings. Then you were allowed to viddy lewdies being shot against walls, officers giving the orders, and also horrible nagoy plotts left lying in gutters, all like cages of bare ribs and white thin nogas. Then there were lewdies being dragged off creeching though not on the sound-track, my brothers, the only sound being music, and being tolchocked while they were dragged off. Then I noticed, in all my pain and sickness, what music it was that like crackled and boomed on the sound-track, and it was Ludwig van, the last movement of the Fifth Symphony, and I creeched like bezoomny at that. 'Stop!' I creeched. 'Stop, you grahzny disgusting sods. It's a sin, that's what it is, a filthy unforgivable sin, you bratchnies!' They didn't stop right away, because there was only a minute or two more to go – lewdies being beaten up and all krovvy, then more firing squads, then the old Nazi flag and THE END. But when the lights came on this Dr Brodsky and also Dr Branom were standing in front of me, and Dr Brodsky said:

'What's all this about sin, eh?'

'That,' I said, very sick. 'Using Ludwig van like that. He did no harm to anyone. Beethoven just wrote music.' And then I was really sick and they had to bring a bowl that was in the shape of like a kidney.

'Music,' said Dr Brodsky, like musing. 'So you're keen on music. I know nothing about it myself. It's a useful emotional heightener, that's all I know. Well, well. What do you think about that, eh, Branom?'

'It can't be helped,' said Dr Branom. 'Each man kills the thing he loves, as the poet-prisoner said. Here's the punishment element, perhaps. The Governor ought to be pleased.'

'Give me a drink,' I said, 'for Bog's sake.'

'Loosen him,' ordered Dr Brodsky. 'Fetch him a carafe of ice-cold water.' So then these under-vecks got to work and soon I was peeting gallons and gallons of water and it was like heaven, O my brothers. Dr Brodsky said:

'You seem a sufficiently intelligent young man. You seem, too, to be not without taste. You've just got this violence thing, haven't you? Violence and theft, theft being an aspect of violence.' I didn't govoreet a single slovo, brothers, I was still feeling sick, though getting a malenky bit better now. But it had been a terrible day. 'Now, then,' said Dr Brodsky, 'how do you think this is done? Tell me, what do you think we're doing to you?'

'You're making me feel ill, I'm ill when I look at those filthy pervert films of yours. But it's not really the films that's doing it. But I feel that if you'll stop these films I'll stop feeling ill.'

'Right,' said Dr Brodsky. 'It's association, the oldest educational method in the world. And what really causes you to feel ill?'

'These grahzny sodding veshches that come out of my gulliver and my plott,' I said, 'that's what it is.'

'Quaint,' said Dr Brodsky, like smiling, 'the dialect of the tribe. Do you know anything of its provenance, Branom?'

'Odd bits of old rhyming slang,' said Dr Branom, who did not look quite so much like a friend any more. 'A bit of gipsy talk, too. But most of the roots are Slav. Propaganda. Subliminal penetration.'

'All right, all right, all right,' said Dr Brodsky, like impatient and not interested any more. 'Well,' he said to me, 'it isn't the wires. It's nothing to do with what's fastened to you. Those are just for measuring your reactions. What is it, then?'

I viddied then, of course, what a bezoomny shoot I was not to notice that it was the hypodermic shots in the rooker. 'Oh,' I creeched, 'oh, I viddy all now. A filthy cally vonny trick. An act of treachery, sod you, and you won't do it again.'

'I'm glad you've raised your objections now,' said Dr Brodsky. 'Now we can be perfectly clear about it. We can get this stuff of Ludovico's into your system in many different ways. Orally, for instance. But the subcutaneous method is the best. Don't fight against it, please. There's no point in your fighting. You can't get the better of us.'

'Grahzny bratchnies,' I said, like snivelling. Then I said: 'I don't mind about the ultra-violence and all that cal. I put up with that. But it's not fair on the music. It's not fair I should feel ill when I'm slooshying lovely Ludwig van and G. F. Handel and others. All that shows you're an evil lot of bastards and I shall never forgive you, sods.'

They both looked a bit like thoughtful. Then Dr Brodsky said: 'Delimitation is always difficult. The world is one, life is one. The sweetest and most heavenly of activities partake in some measure of violence – the act of love, for instance; music, for instance. You must take your chance, boy. The choice has been all yours.' I didn't understand all these slovos, but now I said:

'You needn't take it any further, sir.' I'd changed my tune a malenky bit in my cunning way. 'You've proved to me that all this dratsing and ultra-violence and killing is wrong wrong and terribly wrong. I've learned my lesson, sirs. I see now what I've never seen before. I'm cured, praise God.' And I raised my glazzies in a like holy way to the ceiling. But both these doctors shook their gullivers like sadly and Dr Brodsky said:

'You're not cured yet. There's still a lot to be done. Only when your body reacts promptly and violently to violence, as to a snake, without further help from us, without medication, only then –' I said:

'But, sir, sirs, I *see* that it's wrong. It's wrong because it's against like society, it's wrong because every veck on earth has the right to live and be happy without being beaten and tolchocked and knifed. I've learned a lot, oh really I have.' But Dr Brodsky had a loud long smeck at that, showing all his white zoobies, and said:

'The heresy of an age of reason,' or some such slovos. 'I see what is right and approve, but I do what is wrong. No, no, my boy, you must leave it all to us. But be cheerful about it. It will soon be all over. In less than a fortnight now you'll be a free man.' Then he patted me on the pletcho.

Less than a fortnight. O my brothers and friends, it was like an age. It was like from the beginning of the world to the end of it. To finish the fourteen years without remission in the Staja would have been nothing to it. Every day it was the same. When the devotchka with the hypodermic came round, though, four days after this govoreeting with Dr Brodsky and Dr Branom, I said: 'Oh, no you won't,' and tolchocked her on the rooker, and the syringe went tinkle clatter on to the floor. That was like to viddy what they would do. What they did was to get four or five real bolshy white-coated bastards of under-vecks to hold me down on the bed, tolchocking me with grinny litsos close to mine, and then this nurse ptitsa said: 'You wicked naughty little devil, you,' while she jabbed my rooker with another syringe and squirted this stuff in real brutal and nasty. And then I was wheeled off exhausted to this like hell sinny as before.

Every day, my brothers, these films were like the same, all kicking and tolchocking and red red krovvy dripping off of litsos and plotts and spattering all over the camera lenses. It was usually grinning and smecking malchicks in the heighth of nadsat fashion, or else teeheeheeing Jap torturers or brutal Nazi kickers and shooters. And each day the feeling of wanting to die with the sickness and gulliver pains and aches in the zoobies and horrible horrible thirst grew really worse. Until one morning I tried to defeat the bastards by crash crash crashing my gulliver against the wall so that I should tolchock myself unconscious, but all that happened was I felt sick with viddying that this kind of violence was like the violence in the films, so I was just exhausted and was given the injection and was wheeled off like before.

And then there came a morning when I woke up and had my breakfast of eggs and toast and jam and very hot milky chai, and then I thought: 'It can't be much longer now. Now must be very near the end of the time. I have suffered to the heighths and cannot suffer any more.' And I waited and waited, brothers, for this nurse ptitsa to bring in the syringe, but she did not come. And then the white-coated under-veck came and said:

'Today, old friend, we are letting you walk.'

'Walk?' I said. 'Where?'

'To the usual place,' he said. 'Yes, yes, look not so astonished. You are to walk to the films, me with you of course. You are no longer to be carried in a wheelchair.'

'But,' I said, 'how about my horrible morning injection?' For I was really surprised at this, brothers, they being so keen on pushing this Ludovico veshch into me, as they said. 'Don't I get that horrible sicky stuff rammed into my poor suffering rooker any more?'

'All over,' like smecked this veck. 'For ever and ever amen. You're on your own now, boy. Walking and all to the chamber of horrors. But you're still to be strapped down and made to see. Come on then, my little tiger.' And I had to put my over-gown and toofles on and walk down the corridor to the like sinny metso.

Now this time, O my brothers, I was not only very sick but very puzzled. There it was again, all the old ultra-violence and vecks with their gullivers smashed and torn krovvy-dripping ptitsas creeching for mercy, the like private and individual fillying and nastiness. Then there were the prison-camps and the Jews and the grey like foreign streets full of tanks and uniforms and vecks going down in withering rifle-fire, this being the public side of it. And this time I could blame nothing for me feeling sick and thirsty and full of aches except what I was forced to viddy, my glazzies still being clipped open and my nogas and plott fixed to the chair but this set of wires and other veshches no longer coming out of my plott and gulliver. So what could it be but the films I was viddying that were doing this to me? Except, of course, brothers, that this Ludovico stuff was like a vaccination and there it was cruising about in my krovvy, so that I would be sick always for ever and ever amen whenever I viddied any of this ultra-violence. So now I squared my rot and went boo hoo hoo, and the tears like blotted out what I was forced to viddy in like all blessed runny silvery dewdrops. But these white-coat bratchnies were skorry with their tashtooks to wipe the tears away, saying: 'There there, wazzums all weepy-weepy den.' And there it was again all clear before my glazzies, these Germans prodding like beseeching and weeping Jews – vecks and cheenas and malchicks and devotchkas – into mestos where they would all snuff it of poison gas. Boo hoo hoo I had to go again, and along they came to wipe the tears off, very skorry, so I should not miss one solitary veshch of what they were showing. It was a terrible and horrible day, O my brothers and only friends.

I was lying on the bed all alone that nochy after my dinner of fat thick mutton stew and fruit-pie and ice-cream, and I thought to myself: 'Hell hell hell, there might be a chance for me if I get out now.' I had no weapon, though. I was allowed no britva here, and I had been shaved every other day by a fat bald-headed veck who came to my bed before breakfast, two white-coated bratchnies standing by to viddy I was a good non-violent malchick. The nails on my rookers had been scissored and filed real short so I could not scratch. But I was still skorry on the attack, though they had weakened me down, brothers, to a like shadow of what I had been in the old free days. So now I got off the bed and went to the locked door and began to fist it real horrorshow and hard, creeching at the same time: 'Oh, help help. I'm sick, I'm dying. Doctor doctor doctor, quick. Please. Oh, I'll die, I shall. Help.' My gorlo was real dry and sore before anyone came. Then I heard nogas coming down the corridor and a like grumbling goloss, and then I recognized the goloss of the white-coated veck who brought me pishcha and like escorted me to my daily doom. He like grumbled:

'What is it? What goes on? What's your little nasty game in there?'

'Oh, I'm dying,' I like moaned. 'Oh, I have a ghastly pain in my side. Appendicitis, it is. Ooooooh.'

'Appendy shitehouse,' grumbled this veck, and then to my joy, brothers, I could slooshy the like clank of keys. 'If you're trying it, little friend, my friends and me will beat and kick you all through the night.' Then he opened up and brought in like the sweet air of the promise of my freedom. Now I was like behind the door when he pushed it open, and I could viddy him in the corridor light looking round for me puzzled. Then I raised my two fisties to tolchock him on the neck nasty, and then, I swear, as I sort of viddied him in advance lying moaning or out out out and felt the like joy rise in my guts, it was then that this sickness rose in me as it might be a wave and I felt a horrible fear as if I was really going to die. I like tottered over to the bed going urgh urgh urgh, and the veck, who was not in his white coat but an over-gown, viddied clear enough what I had had in my mind for he said:

'Well, everything's a lesson, isn't it? Learning all the time, as you could say. Come on, little friend, get up from that bed and hit me. I want you to, yes, really. A real good crack across the jaw. Oh, I'm dying for it, really I am.' But all I could do, brothers, was to just lay there sobbing boo hoo hoo. 'Scum,' like sneered this veck now. 'Filth.' And he pulled me up by like the scruff of my pyjama-top, me being very weak and limp, and he raised and swung his right rooker so that I got a fair old tolchock clean on the litso. 'That,' he said, 'is for getting me out of my bed, you young dirt.' And he wiped his rookers against each other swish swish and went out. Crunch crunch went the key in the lock.

And what, brothers, I had to escape into sleep from then was the horrible and wrong feeling that it was better to get the hit than give it. If that veck had stayed I might even have like presented the other cheek.

# 7

I could not believe, brothers, what I was told. It seemed that I had been in that vonny mesto for near ever and would be there for near ever more. But it had always been a fortnight and now they said the fortnight was near up. They said:

'Tomorrow, little friend, out out out.' And they made with the old thumb, like pointing to freedom. And then the white-coated veck who had tolchocked me and who had still brought me my trays of pishcha and like escorted me to my everyday torture said: 'But you still have one real big day in front of you. It's to be your passing-out day,' and he had a leery smeck at that.

I expected this morning that I would be ittying as usual to the sinny mesto in my pyjamas and toofles and over-gown. But no. This morning I was given my shirt and underveshches and my platties of the night and my horrorshow kick-boots, all lovely and washed or ironed and polished. And I was even given my cut-throat britva that I had used in those old happy days for fillying and dratsing. So I gave with the puzzled frown at this as I got dressed, but the white-coated under-veck just like grinned and would govoreet nothing, O my brothers.

I was led quite kindly to the same old mesto, but there were changes there. Curtains had been drawn in front of the sinny screen and the frosted glass under the projection holes was no longer there, it having perhaps been pushed up or folded to the sides like blinds or shutters. And where there had been just the noise of coughing kashl kashl kashl and like shadows of the lewdies was now a real audience, and in this audience there were litsos I knew. There was the Staja Governor and the holy man, the charlie or charles as he was called, and the Chief Chasso and this very important and well-dressed chelloveck who was the Minister of the Interior or Inferior. All the rest I did not know. Dr Brodsky and Dr Branom were there, though not now white-coated, instead they were dressed as doctors would dress who were big enough to want to dress in the heighth of fashion. Dr Branom just stood, but Dr Brodsky stood and govoreeted in a like learned manner to all the lewdies assembled. When he viddied me coming in he said: 'Aha. At this stage, gentlemen, we introduce the subject himself. He is, as you will perceive, fit and well nourished. He comes straight from a night's sleep and a good breakfast, undrugged, unhypnotized. Tomorrow we send him with confidence out into the world again, as decent a lad as you would meet on a May morning, inclined to the kindly word and the helpful act. What a change is here, gentlemen, from the wretched hoodlum the State committed to unprofitable punishment some two years ago, unchanged after two years. Unchanged, do I say? Not quite. Prison taught him the false smile, the rubbed hands of hypocrisy, the fawning greased obsequious leer. Other vices it taught him, as well as confirming him in those he had long practised before. But, gentlemen, enough of words. Actions speak louder than. Action now. Observe, all.'

I was a bit dazed by all this govoreeting and I was trying to grasp in my mind that like all this was about me. Then all the lights went out and then there came on two like spotlights shining from the projection-squares, and one of them was full on Your Humble and Suffering Narrator. And into the other spotlight there walked a bolshy big chelloveck I had never viddied before. He had a lardy like litso and a moustache and like strips of hair pasted over his near-bald gulliver. He was about thirty or forty or fifty, some old age like that, starry. He ittied up to me and the spotlight ittied with him, and soon the two spotlights had made like one big pool. He said to me, very sneery: 'Hello, heap of dirt. Pooh, you don't wash much, judging from the horrible smell.' Then, as if he was like dancing, he stamped on my nogas, left, right, then he gave me a finger-nail flick on the nose that hurt like bezoomny and brought the old tears to my glazzies then he twisted at my left ooko like it was a radio dial. I could slooshy titters and a couple of real horrorshow hawhawhaws coming from like the audience. My nose and nogas and ear-hole stung and pained like bezoomny, so I said:

'What do you do that to me for? I've never done wrong to you, brother.'

'Oh,' this veck said, 'I do this' – flickedflicked nose again – 'and that' – twisted smarting ear-hole – 'and the other' – stamped nasty on right noga – 'because I don't care for your horrible type. And if you want to do anything about it, start, start, please do.' Now I knew that I'd have to be real skorry and get my cut-throat britva out before this horrible killing sickness whooshed up and turned the like joy of battle into feeling I was going to snuff it. But, O brothers, as my rooker reached for the britva in my inside carman I got this like picture in my mind's glazzy of this insulting chelloveck howling for mercy with the red red krovvy all streaming out of his rot, and hot after this picture the sickness and dryness and pains were rushing to overtake, and I viddied that I'd have to change the way I felt about this rotten veck very very skorry indeed, so I felt in my carmans for cigarettes or for pretty polly, and, O my brothers, there was not either of these veshches. I said, like all howly and blubbery:

'I'd like to give you a cigarette, brother, but I don't seem to have any.' This veck went:

'Wah wah. Boohoohoo. Cry, baby.' Then he flick-flickflicked with his bolshy horny nail at my nose again, and I could slooshy very loud smecks of like mirth coming from the dark audience. I said, real desperate, trying to be nice to this insulting and hurtful veck to stop the pains and sickness coming up:

'Please let me do something for you, please.' And I felt in my carmans but could find only my cut-throat britva, so I took this out and handed it to him and said: 'Please take this, please. A little present. Please have it.' But he said:

'Keep your stinking bribes to yourself. You can't get round me that way.' And he banged at my rooker and my cut-throat britva fell on the floor. So I said:

'Please, I must do something. Shall I clean your boots? Look, I'll get down and lick them.' And, my brothers, believe it or kiss my sharries, I got down on my knees and pushed my red yahzick out a mile and half to lick his grahzny vonny boots. But all this veck did was to kick me not too hard on the rot. So then it seemed to me that it would not bring on the sickness and pain if I just gripped his ankles with my rookers tight round them and brought this grashzny bratchny down to the floor. So I did this and he got a real bolshy surprise, coming down crack amid loud laughter from the vonny audience. But viddying him on the floor I could feel the whole horrible feeling coming over me, so I gave him my rooker to lift him up skorry and up he came. Then just as he was going to give me a real nasty and earnest tolchock on the litso Dr Brodsky said:

'All right, that will do very well.' Then this horrible veck sort of bowed and danced off like an actor while the lights came up on me blinking and with my rot square for howling. Dr Brodsky said to the audience: 'Our subject is, you see, impelled towards the good by, paradoxically, being impelled towards evil. The intention to act violently is accompanied by strong feelings of physical distress. To counter these the subject has to switch to a diametrically opposed attitude. Any questions?'

'Choice,' rumbled a rich deep goloss. I viddied it belonged to the prison charlie. 'He has no real choice, has he? Self-interest, fear of physical pain, drove him to that grotesque act of self-abasement. Its insincerity was clearly to be seen. He ceases to be a wrongdoer. He ceases also to be a creature capable of moral choice.'

'These are subtleties,' like smiled Dr Brodsky. 'We are not concerned with motive, with the higher ethics. We are concerned only with cutting down crime –'

'And,' chipped in this bolshy well-dressed Minister, 'with relieving the ghastly congestion in our prisons.'

'Hear hear,' said somebody.

There was a lot of govoreeting and arguing then and I just stood there, brothers, like completely ignored by all these ignorant bratchnies, so I creeched out:

'Me, me, me. How about me? Where do I come into all this? Am I like just some animal or dog?' And that started them off govoreeting real loud and throwing slovos at me. So I creeched louder, still creeching: 'Am I just to be like a clock-work orange?' I didn't know what made me use those slovos, brothers, which just came like without asking into my gulliver. And that shut all those vecks up for some reason for a minoota or two. Then one very thin starry professor type chelloveck stood up, his neck like all cables carrying like power from his gulliver to his plott, and he said:

'You have no cause to grumble, boy. You made your choice and all this is a consequence of your choice. Whatever now ensues is what you yourself have chosen.' And the prison charlie creeched out:

'Oh, if only I could believe that.' And you could viddy the Governor give him a look like meaning that he would not climb so high in like Prison Religion as he thought he would. Then loud arguing started again, and then I could slooshy the slovo Love being thrown around, the prison charles himself creeching as loud as any about Perfect Love Casteth Out Fear and all that cal. And now Dr Brodsky said, smiling all over his litso:

'I am glad, gentlemen, this question of Love has been raised. Now we shall see in action a manner of Love that was thought to be dead with the Middle Ages.' And then the lights went down and the spotlights came on again, one on your poor and suffering Friend and Narrator, and into the other there like rolled or sidled the most lovely young devotchka you could ever hope in all your jeezny, O my brothers, to viddy. That is to say, she had real horrorshow groodies all of which you could like viddy, she having on platties which came down down down off her pletchoes. And her nogas were like Bog in His Heaven, and she walked like to make you groan in your keeshkas, and yet her litso was a sweet smiling young like innocent litso. She came up towards me with the light like it was the like light of heavenly grace and all that cal coming with her, and the first thing that flashed into my gulliver was that I would like to have her right down there on the floor with the old in-out real savage, but skorry as a shot came the sickness, like a like detective that had been watching round a corner and now followed to make his grahzny arrest. And now the von of lovely perfume that came off her made me want to think of starting to like heave in my keeshkas, so I knew I had to think of some new like way of thinking about her before all the pain and thirstiness and horrible sickness come over me real horrorshow and proper. So I creeched out:

'O most beautiful and beauteous of devotchkas, I throw like my heart at your feet for you to like trample all over. If I had a rose I would give it to you. If it was all rainy and cally now on the ground you could have my platties to walk on so as not to cover your dainty nogas with filth and cal.' And as I was saying all this, O my brothers, I could feel the sickness like slinking back. 'Let me,' I creeched out, 'worship you and be like your helper and protector from the wicked like world.' Then I thought of the right slovo and felt better for it, saying: 'Let me be like your true knight,' and down I went again on the old knees, bowing and like scraping.

And then I felt real shooty and dim, it having been like an act again, for this devotchka smiled and bowed to the audience and like danced off, the lights coming up to a bit of applause. And the glazzies of some of these starry vecks in the audience were like popping out at this young devotchka with dirty and like unholy desire, O my brothers.

'He will be your true Christian,' Dr Brodsky was creeching out, 'ready to turn the other cheek, ready to be crucified rather than crucify, sick to the very heart at the thought even of killing a fly.' And that was right, brothers, because when he said that I thought of killing a fly and felt just that tiny bit sick, but I pushed the sickness and pain back by thinking of the fly being fed with bits of sugar and looked after like a bleeding pet and all that cal. 'Reclamation,' he creeched. 'Joy before the Angels of God.'

'The point is,' this Minister of the Inferior was saying real gromky, 'that it works.'

'Oh,' the prison charlie said, like sighing, 'it works all right, God help the lot of us.'

# Part Three

## 1

'What's it going to be then, eh?'

That, my brothers, was me asking myself the next morning, standing outside this white building that was like tacked on to the old Staja, in my platties of the night of two years back in the grey light of dawn, with a malenky bit of a bag with my few personal veshches in and a bit of cutter kindly donated by the vonny Authorities to like start me off in my new life.

The rest of the day before had been very tiring, what with interviews to go on tape for the telenews and photographs being took flash flash flash and more like demonstrations of me folding up in the face of ultra-violence and all that embarrassing cal. And then I had like fallen into the bed and then, as it looked to me, been waked up to be told to get off out, to itty off home, they did not want to viddy Your Humble Narrator never not no more, O my brothers. So there I was, very very early in the morning, with just this bit of pretty polly in my left carman, jingle-jangling it and wondering:

'What's it going to be then, eh?'

Some breakfast some mesto, I thought, me not having eaten at all that morning, every veck being so anxious to tolchock me off out to freedom. A chasha of chai only I had peeted. This Staja was in a very like gloomy part of the town, but there were malenky workers' caffs all around and I soon found one of those, my brothers. It was very cally and vonny, with one bulb in the ceiling with fly-dirt like obscuring its bit of light, and there were early rabbiters slurping away at chai and horrible-looking sausages and slices of kleb which they like wolfed, going wolf wolf wolf and then creeching for more. They were served by a very cally devotchka but with very bolshy groodies on her, and some of the eating vecks tried to grab her, going haw haw haw while she went he he he, and the sight of them near made me want to sick, brothers. But I asked for some toast and jam and chai very politely and with my gentleman's goloss, then I sat in a dark corner to eat and peet.

While I was doing this, a malenky little dwarf of a veck ittied in, selling the morning's gazettas, a twisted and grahzny prestoopnick type with thick glasses on with steel rims, his platties like the colour of very starry decaying currant pudding. I kupetted a gazetta, my idea being to get ready for plunging back into normal jeezny again by viddying what was ittying on in the world. This gazetta I had seemed to be like a Government gazetta, for the only news that was on the front page was about the need for every veck to make sure he put the Government back in again on the next General Election, which seemed to be about two or three weeks off. There were very boastful slovos about what the Government had done, brothers, in the last year or so, what with increased exports and a real horrorshow foreign policy and improved social services and all that cal. But what the Government was really most boastful about was the way in which they reckoned the streets had been made safer for all peace-loving night-walking lewdies in the last six months, what with better pay for the police and the police getting like tougher with young hooligans and perverts and burglars and all that cal. Which interessovatted Your Humble Narrator some deal. And on the second page of the gazetta there was a blurry like photograph of somebody who looked very familiar, and it turned out to be none other than me me me. I looked very gloomy and like scared, but that was really with the flashbulbs going pop pop all the time. What it said underneath my picture was that here was the first graduate from the new State Institute for Reclamation of Criminal Types, cured of his criminal instincts in a fortnight only, now a good law-fearing citizen and all that cal. Then I viddied there was a very boastful article about this Ludovico's Technique and how clever the Government was and all that cal. Then there was another picture of some veck I thought I knew, and it was this Minister of the Inferior or Interior. It seemed that he had been doing a bit of boasting, looking forward to a nice crime-free era in which there would be no more fear of cowardly attacks from young hooligans and perverts and burglars and all that cal. So I went arghhhhhh and threw this gazetta on the floor, so that it covered up stains of spilled chai and horrible spat gobs from the cally animals that used this caff.

'What's it going to be then, eh?'

What it was going to be now, brothers, was homeways and a nice surprise for dadada and mum, their only son and heir back in the family bosom. Then I could lay back on the bed in my own malenky den and slooshy some lovely music, and at the same time I could think over what to do now with my jeezny. The Discharge Officer had given me a long list the day before of jobs I could try for, and he had telephoned to different vecks about me, but I had no intention, my brothers, of going off to rabbit right away. A malenky bit of a rest first, yes, and a quiet think on the bed to the sound of lovely music.

And so the autobus to Center, and then the autobus to Kingsley Avenue, the flats of Flatblock 18A being just near. You will believe me, my brothers, when I say that my heart was going clopclopclop with the like excitement. All was very quiet, it still being early winter morning, and when I ittied into the vestibule of the flatblock there was no veck about, only the nagoy vecks and cheenas of the Dignity of Labour. What surprised me, brothers, was the way that had been cleaned up, there being no longer any dirty ballooning slovos from the rots of the Dignified Labourers, not any dirty parts of the body added to their naked plotts by dirty-minded pencilling malchicks. And what also surprised me was that the lift was working. It came purring down when I pressed the electric knopka, and when I got in I was surprised again to viddy all was clean inside the like cage.

So up I went to the tenth floor, and there I saw 10–8 as it had been before, and my rooker trembled and shook as I took out of my carman the little klootch I had for opening up. But I very firmly fitted the klootch in the lock and turned, then opened up then went in, and there I met three pairs of surprised and almost frightened glazzies looking at me, and it was pee and em having their breakfast, but it was also another veck that I had never viddied in my jeezny before, a bolshy thick veck in his shirt and braces, quite at home, brothers, slurping away at the milky chai and munchmunching at his eggiweg and toast. And it was this stranger veck who spoke first, saying:

'Who are you, friend? Where did you get hold of a key? Out, before I push your face in. Get out there and knock. Explain your business, quick.'

My dad and mum sat like petrified, and I could viddy they had not yet read the gazetta, then I remembered that the gazetta did not arrive till papapa had gone off to his work. But then mum said: 'Oh, you've broken out. You've escaped. Whatever shall we do? We shall have the police here, oh oh oh. Oh, you bad and wicked boy, disgracing us all like this.' And, believe it or kiss my sharries, she started to go boo hoo. So I started to try and explain, they could ring up the Staja if they wanted, and all the time this stranger veck sat there like frowning and looking as if he could push my litso in with his hairy bolshy beefy fist. So I said:

'How about you answering a few, brother? What are you doing here and for how long? I didn't like the tone of what you said just then. Watch it. Come on, speak up.' He was a working-man type veck, very ugly, about thirty or forty, and he sat now with his rot open at me, not govoreeting one single slovo. Then my dad said:

'This is all a bit bewildering, son. You should have let us know you were coming. We thought it would be at least another five or six years before they let you out. Not,' he said, and he said it very like gloomy, 'that we're not very pleased to see you again and a free man, too.'

'Who is this?' I said. 'Why can't he speak up? What's going on in here?'

'This is Joe,' said my mum. 'He lives here now. The lodger, that's what he is. Oh, dear dear dear,' she went.

'You,' said this Joe. 'I've heard all about you, boy. I know what you've done, breaking the hearts of your poor grieving parents. So you're back, eh? Back to make life a misery for them once more, is that it? Over my dead corpse you will, because they've let me be more like a son to them than like a lodger.' I could nearly have smecked loud at that if the old razdraz within me hadn't started to wake up the feeling of wanting to sick, because this veck looked about the same age as my pee and em, and there he was like trying to put a son's protecting rooker round my crying mum, O my brothers.

'So,' I said, and I near felt like collapsing in all tears myself. 'So that's it, then. Well, I give you five large minootas to clear all your horrible cally veshches out of my room.' And I made for this room, this veck being a malenky bit too slow to stop me. When I opened the door my heart cracked to the carpet, because I viddied it was no longer like my room at all, brothers. All my flags had gone off the walls and this veck had put up pictures of boxers, also like a team sitting smug with folded rookers and silver like shield in front. And then I viddied what else was missing. My stereo and my disc-cupboard were no longer there, nor was my locked treasure-chest that contained bottles and drugs and two shining clean syringes. 'There's been some filthy vonny work going on here,' I creeched. 'What have you done with my own personal vesches, you horrible bastard?' This was to this Joe, but it was my dad that answered, saying:

'That was all took away, son, by the police. This new regulation, see, about compensation for the victims.'

I found it very hard not to be very ill, but my gulliver was aching shocking and my rot was so dry that I had to take a skorry swig from the milk-bottle on the table, so that this Joe said: 'Filthy piggish manners.' I said:

'But she died. That one died.'

'It was the cats, son,' said my dad like sorrowful, 'that were left with nobody to look after them till the will was read, so they had to have somebody in to feed them. So the police sold your things, clothes and all, to help with the looking after of them. That's the law, son. But you were never much of a one for following the law.'

I had to sit down then, and this Joe said: 'Ask permission before you sit, you mannerless young swine,' so I cracked back skorry with a 'Shut your dirty big fat hole, you,' feeling sick. Then I tried to be all reasonable and smiling for my health's sake like, so I said: 'Well, that's my room, there's no denying that. This is my home also. What suggestions have you, my pee and em, to make?' But they just looked very glum, my mum shaking a bit, her litso all lines and wet with like tears, and then my dad said:

'All this needs thinking about, son. We can't very well just kick Joe out, not just like that, can we? I mean, Joe's here doing a job, a contract it is, two years, and we made like an arrangement, didn't we, Joe? I mean, son, thinking you were going to stay in prison a long time and that room going begging.' He was a bit ashamed, you could viddy that from his litso. So I just smiled and like nodded, saying:

'I viddy all. You got used to a bit of peace and you got used to a bit of extra pretty polly. That's the way it goes. And your son has just been nothing but a terrible nuisance.' And then, my brothers, believe me or kiss my sharries, I started to like cry, feeling very like sorry for myself. So my dad said:

'Well, you see, son, Joe's paid next month's rent already. I mean, whatever we do in the future we can't say to Joe to get out, can we, Joe?' This Joe said:

'It's you two I've got to think of, who've been like a father and mother to me. Would it be right or fair to go off and leave you to the tender mercies of this young monster who has been like no real son at all? He's weeping now, but that's his craft and artfulness. Let him go off and find a room somewhere. Let him learn the error of his ways and that a bad boy like he's been doesn't deserve such a good mum and dad as what he's had.'

'All right,' I said, standing up in all like tears still. 'I know how things are now. Nobody wants or loves me. I've suffered and suffered and suffered and everybody wants me to go on suffering. I know.'

'You've made others suffer,' said this Joe. 'It's only right you should suffer proper. I've been told everything that you've done, sitting here at night round the family table, and pretty shocking it was to listen to. Made me real sick a lot of it did.'

'I wish,' I said, 'I was back in the prison. Dear old Staja as it was. I'm ittying off now,' I said. 'You won't ever viddy me no more. I'll make my own way, thank you very much. Let it lie heavy on your consciences.' My dad said:

'Don't take it like that, son,' and my mum just went boo hoo hoo, her litso all screwed up real ugly, and this Joe put his rooker round her again, patting her and going there there there like bezoomny. And so I just sort of staggered to the door and went out, leaving them to their horrible guilt, O my brothers.

2

Ittying down the street in a like aimless sort of a way brothers, in these night platties which lewdies like stared at as I went by, cold too, it being a bastard cold winter day, all I felt I wanted was to be away from all this and not have to think any more about any sort of veshch at all. So I got the autobus to Center, then walked back to Taylor Place, and there was the disc-bootick MELODIA—I had used to favour with my inestimable custom, O my brothers, and it looked much the same sort of mesto as it always had, and walking in I expected to viddy old Andy there, that bald and very very thin helpful little veck from whom I had kupetted discs in the old days. But there was no Andy there now, brothers, only a scream and a creech of nadsat (teenage, that is) malchicks and ptitsas slooshying some new horrible popsong and dancing to it as well, and the veck behind the counter not much more than a nadsat himself, clicking his rooker-bones and smecking like bezoomny. So I went up and waited till he like deigned to notice me, then I said:

'I'd like to hear a disc of the Mozart Number Forty.' I don't know why that should have come into my gulliver, but it did. The counter-veck said:

'Forty what, friend?'

I said: 'Symphony. Symphony Number Forty in G Minor.'

'Ooooh,' went one of the dancing nadsats, a malchick with his hair all over his glazzies, 'seemfunnah. Don't it seem funny? He wants a seemfunnah.'

I could feel myself growing all razdraz within, but I had to watch that, so I like smiled at the veck who had taken over Andy's place and at all the dancing and creeching nadsats. This counter-veck said: 'You go into that listen-booth over there, friend, and I'll pipe something through.'

So I went over to the malenky box where you could slooshy the discs you wanted to buy, and then this veck put a disc on for me, but it wasn't the Mozart Forty, it was the Mozart 'Prague' – he seemingly having just picked up any Mozart he could find on the shelf – and that should have started making me real razdraz and I had to watch that for fear of the pain and sickness, but what I'd forgotten was something I shouldn't have forgotten and now made me want to snuff it. It was that these doctor bratchnies had so fixed things that any music that was like for the emotions would make me sick just like viddying or wanting to do violence. It was because all those violence films had music with them. And I remembered especially that horrible Nazi film with the Beethoven Fifth, last movement. And now here was lovely Mozart made horrible. I dashed out of the shop with these nadsats smecking after me and the counter-veck creeching: 'Eh eh eh!' But I took no notice and went staggering almost like blind across the road and round the corner to the Korova Milkbar. I knew what I wanted.

The mesto was near empty, it being still morning. It looked strange too, having been painted with all red mooing cows, and behind the counter was no veck I knew. But when I said: 'Milk plus, large,' the veck with a like lean litso very newly shaved knew what I wanted. I took the large moloko plus to one of the little cubies that were all round this mesto, there being like curtains to shut them off from the main mesto, and there I sat down in the plushy chair and sipped and sipped. When I'd finished the whole lot I began to feel that things were happening. I had my glazzies like fixed on a malenky bit of silver paper from a cancer packet that was on the floor, the sweeping-up of this mesto not being all that horrorshow, brothers. This scrap of silver began to grow and grow and grow and it was so like bright and fiery that I had to squint my glazzies at it. It got so big that it became not only this whole cubie I was lolling in but like the whole Korova, the whole street, the whole city. Then it was the whole world, then it was the whole everything, brothers, and it was like a sea washing over every veshch that had ever been made or thought of even. I could sort of slooshy myself making special sort of shooms and govoreeting slovos like 'Dear dead idlewilds, rot not in variform guises' and all that cal. Then I could like feel the vision beating up in all this silver, and then there were colours like nobody had ever viddied before, and then I could viddy like a group of statues a long long long way off that was like being pushed nearer and nearer and nearer, all lit up by very bright light from below and above alike, O my brothers. This group of statues was of God or Bog and all His Holy Angels and Saints, all very bright like bronze, with beards and bolshy great wings that waved about in a kind of wind, so that they could not really be of stone or bronze, really, and the eyes or glazzies like moved and were alive. These bolshy big figures came nearer and nearer and nearer till they were like going to crush me down, and I could slooshy my goloss going 'Eeeeee'. And I felt I had got rid of everything – platties, body, brain, name, the lot – and felt real horrorshow, like in heaven. Then there was the shoom of like crumbling and crumpling, and Bog and the Angels and Saints sort of shook their gullivers at me, as though to govoreet that there wasn't quite time now but I must try again, and then everything like leered and smecked and collapsed and the big warm light grew like cold, and then there I was as I was before, the empty glass on the table and wanting to cry and feeling like death was the only answer to everything.

And that was it, that was what I viddied quite clear was the thing to do, but how to do it I did not properly know, never having thought of that before, O my brothers. In my little bag of personal veshches I had my cut-throat britva, but I at once felt very sick as I thought of myself going swishhhh at myself and all my own red red krovvy flowing. What I wanted was not something violent but something that would make me like just go off gentle to sleep and that be the end of Your Humble Narrator, no more trouble to anybody any more. Perhaps, I thought, if I ittied off to the Public Biblio around the corner I might find some book on the best way of snuffing it with no pain. I thought of myself dead and how sorry everybody was going to be, pee and em and that cally vonny Joe who was a like usurper, and also Dr Brodsky and Dr Branom and that Inferior Interior Minister and every veck else. And the boastful vonny Government too. So out I scatted into the winter, and it was afternoon now, near two o'clock, as I could viddy from the bolshy Center timepiece, so that me being in the land with the old moloko plus must have took like longer than

I thought. I walked down Marghanita Boulevard and then turned into Boothby Avenue, then round the corner again, and there was the Public Biblio.

It was a starry cally sort of a mesto that I could not remember going into since I was a very very malenky malchick, no more than about six years old, and there were two parts of it – one part to borrow books and one part to read in, full of gazettas and mags and like the von of very starry old men with their plotts stinking of like old age and poverty. These were standing at the gazetta stands all round the room, sniffling and belching and govoreeting to themselves and turning over the pages to read the news very sadly, or else they were sitting at the tables looking at the mags or pretending to, some of them asleep and one or two of them snoring real gromky. I couldn't like remember what it was I wanted at first, then I remembered with a bit of shock that I had ittied here to find out how to snuff it without pain, so I goolied over to the shelf full of reference veshches. There were a lot of books, but there was none with a title, brothers, that would really do. There was a medical book that I took down, but when I opened it it was full of drawings and photographs of horrible wounds and diseases, and that made me want to sick just a bit. So I put that back and then took down the big book or Bible, as it was called, thinking that might give me like comfort as it had done in the old Staja days (not so old really, but it seemed a very very long time ago), and I staggered over to a chair to read in it. But all I found was about smiting seventy times seven and a lot of Jews cursing and tolchocking each other, and that made me want to sick, too. So then I near cried, so that a very starry ragged moodge opposite me said:

'What is it, son? What's the trouble?'

'I want to snuff it,' I said. 'I've had it, that's what it is. Life's become too much for me.'

A starry reading veck next to me said: 'Shhhh,' without looking up from some bezoomny mag he had full of drawings of like bolshy geometrical veshches. That rang a bell somehow. This other moodge said:

'You're too young for that, son. Why, you've got everything in front of you.'

'Yes,' I said, bitter. 'Like a pair of false groodies.' This mag-reading veck said: 'Shhhh' again, looking up this time, and something clocked for both of us. I viddied who it was. He said, real gromky:

'I never forget a shape, by God. I never forget the shape of anything. By God, you young swine, I've got you now.' Crystallography, that was it. That was what he'd been taking away from the Biblio that time. False teeth crunched up real horrorshow. Platties torn off. His books razrezzed, all about Crystallography. I thought I had best get out of here real skorry, brothers. But this starry old moodge was on his feet, creeching like bezoomny to all the starry old coughers at the gazettas round the walls and to them dozing over mags at the tables. 'We have him,' he creeched. 'The poisonous young swine who ruined the books on Crystallography, rare books, books not to be obtained ever again, anywhere.' This had a terrible mad shoom about it, as though this old veck was really off his gulliver. 'A prize specimen of the cowardly brutal young,' he creeched. 'Here in our midst and at our mercy. He and his friends beat me and kicked me and thumped me. They stripped me and tore out my teeth. They laughed at my blood and my moans. They kicked me off home, dazed and naked.' All this wasn't quite true, as you know, brothers. He had some platties on, he hadn't been completely nagoy.

I creeched back: 'That was over two years ago. I've been punished since then. I've learned my lesson. See over there – my picture's in the papers.'

'Punishment, eh?' said one starry like ex-soldier type. 'You lot should be exterminated. Like so many noisome pests. Punishment, indeed.'

'All right, all right,' I said. 'Everybody's entitled to his opinion. Forgive me, all. I must go now.' And I started to itty out of this mesto of bezoomny old men. Aspirin, that was it. You could snuff it on a hundred aspirin. Aspirin from the old drugstore. But the crystallography veck creeched:

'Don't let him go. We'll teach him all about punishment, the murderous young pig. Get him.' And, believe it, brothers, or do the other veshch, two or three starry dodderers, about ninety years old apiece, grabbed me with their trembly old rookers, and I was like made sick by the von of old age and disease which came from these near-dead moodges. The crystal veck was on to me now, starting to deal me malenky weak tolchocks on my litso, and I tried to get away and itty out, but these starry rookers that held me were stronger than I had thought. Then other starry vecks came hobbling from the gazettas to have a go at Your Humble Narrator. They were creeching veshches like: 'Kill him, stamp on him, murder him, kick his teeth in,' and all that cal. and I could viddy what it was clear enough. It was old age having a go at youth, that's what it was. But some of them were saying: 'Poor old Jack, near killed poor old Jack he did, this is the young swine' and so on, as though it had all happened yesterday. Which to them I suppose it had. There was now like a sea of vonny runny dirty old men trying to get at me with their like feeble rookers and horny old claws; creeching and panting on to me, but our crystal droog was there in front, dealing out tolchock after tolchock. And I daren't do a solitary single veshch, O my brothers, it being better to be hit at like that than to want to sick and feel that horrible pain, but of course the fact that there was violence going on made me feel that the sickness was peeping round the corner to viddy whether to come out into the open and roar away.

Then an attendant veck came along, a youngish veck, and he creeched: 'What goes on here? Stop it at once. This is a reading-room.' But nobody took any notice. So the attendant veck said: 'Right, I shall phone the police.' So I creeched, and I never thought I would ever do that in all my jeezny:

'Yes yes yes, do that, protect me from these old madmen.' I noticed that the attendant veck was not too anxious to join in the dratsing and rescue me from the rage and madness of these starry vecks' claws; he just scatted off to his like office or wherever the telephone was. Now these old men were panting a lot now, and I felt I could just flick at them and they would all fall over, but I just let myself be held, very patient, by these starry rookers, my glazzies closed, and feel the feeble tolchocks on my litso, also slooshy the panting breathy old golosses creeching: 'Young swine, young murderer, hooligan, thug, kill him.' Then I got such a real painful tolchock on the nose that I said to myself to hell to hell, and I opened my glazzies up and started to struggle to get free, which was not hard, brothers, and I tore off creeching to the sort of hallway outside the reading-room. But these starry avengers still came after me, panting like dying, with their animal claws all trembling to get at your friend and Humble Narrator. Then I was tripped up and was on the floor and was being kicked at, then I slooshied golosses of young vecks creeching: 'All right, all right, stop it now,' and I knew the police had arrived.

## 3

I was like dazed, O my brothers, and could not viddy very clear, but I was sure I had met these millicents some mesto before. The one who had hold of me, going: 'There there there,' just by the front door of the Public Biblio, him I did not know at all, but it seemed to me he was like very young to be a rozz. But the other two had backs that I was sure I had viddied before. They were lashing into these starry old vecks with great bolshy glee and joy, swishing away with malenky whips, creeching: 'There, you naughty boys. That should teach you to stop rioting and breaking the State's Peace, you wicked villains, you.' So they drove these panting and wheezing and near dying starry avengers back into the reading-room, then they turned round, smecking with the fun they'd had, to viddy me. The older one of the two said:

'Well well well well well well well. If it isn't little Alex. Very long time no viddy, droog. How goes?' I was like dazed, the uniform and the shlem or helmet making it hard to viddy who this was, though litso and goloss were very familiar. Then I looked at the other one, and about him, with his grinning bezoomny litso, there was no doubt. Then, all numb and growing number. I looked back at the well well welling one. This one was then fatty old Billyboy, my old enemy. The other was, of course, Dim, who had used to be my droog and also the enemy of stinking fatty goaty Billyboy, but was now a millicent with uniform and shlem and whip to keep order. I said:

'Oh no.'

'Surprise, eh?' And old Dim came out with the old guff. I remembered so horrorshow: 'Huh huh huh.'

'It's impossible,' I said. 'It can't be so. I don't believe it.'

'Evidence of the old glazzies,' grinned Billyboy. 'Nothing up our sleeves. No magic, droog. A job for two who are now of job-age. The police.'

'You're too young,' I said. 'Much too young. They don't make rozzes of malchicks of your age.'

'Was young,' went old millicent Dim. I could not get over it, brothers, I really could not. 'That's what we was, young droogie. And you it was that was always the youngest. And here now we are.'

'I still can't believe it,' I said. Then Billyboy, rozz Billyboy that I couldn't get over, said to this young millicent that was like holding on to me and that I did not know:

'More good would be done, I think, Rex, if we doled out a bit of the old summary. Boys will be boys, as always was. No need to go through the old station routine. This one here has been up to his old tricks, as we can well remember though you, of course, can't. He has been attacking the aged and defenceless, and they have properly been retaliating. But we must have our say in the State's name.'

'What is all this?' I said, not able hardly to believe my ookos. 'It was them that went for me, brothers. You're not on their side and can't be. You can't be, Dim. It was a veck we fillied with once in the old days trying to get his own malenky bit of revenge after all this long time.'

'Long time is right,' said Dim. 'I don't remember them days too horrorshow. Don't call me Dim no more, either. Officer call me.'

'Enough is remembered, though,' Billyboy kept nodding. He was not so fatty as he had been. 'Naughty little malchicks handy with cut-throat britvas – these must be kept under.' And they took me in a real strong grip and like walked me out of the Biblio. There was a millicent patrol-car waiting outside, and this veck they called Rex was the driver. They like tolchocked me into the back of this auto, and I couldn't help feeling it was all really like a joke, and that Dim anyway would pull his shlem off his gulliver and go haw haw haw. But he didn't. I said, trying to fight the strack inside me:

'And old Pete, what happened to old Pete? It was sad about Georgie,' I said. 'I slooshied all about that.'

'Pete, oh yes, Pete,' said Dim. 'I seem to remember like the name.' I could viddy we were driving out of town. I said:

'Where are we supposed to be going?'

Billyboy turned round from the front to say: 'It's light still. A little drive into the country, all winter-bare but lonely and lovely. It is not right, not always, for lewdies in the town to viddy too much of our summary punishment. Streets must be kept clean in more than one way.' And he turned to the front again.

'Come,' I said. 'I just don't get this at all. The old days are dead and gone days. For what I did in the past I have been punished. I have been cured.'

'That was read out to us,' said Dim. 'The Super read all that out to us. He said it was a very good way.'

'Read to you,' I said, a malenky bit nasty. 'You still too dim to read for yourself, O brother?'

'Ah, no,' said Dim, very like gentle and like regretful. 'Not to speak like that. Not no more, droogie.' And he launched a bolshy tolchock right on my cluve, so that all red red nose-krovvy started to drip drip drip.

'There was never any trust,' I said, bitter, wiping off the krovvy with my rooker. 'I was always on my oddy knocky.'

'This will do,' said Billyboy. We were now in the country and it was all bare trees and a few odd distant like twitters, and in the distance there was some like farm machine making a whirring schoom. It was getting all dusk now, this being the height of winter. There were no lewdies about, nor no animals. There was just the four. 'Get out, Alex boy,' said Dim. 'Just a malenky bit of summary.'

All through what they did this driver veck just sat at the wheel of the auto, smoking a cancer, reading a malenky bit of a book. He had the light on in the auto to viddy by. He took no notice of what Billyboy and Dim did to your Humble Narrator. I will not go into what they did, but it was all like panting and thudding against this like background of whirring farm engines and the twittwittwittering in the bare or nagoy branches. You could viddy a bit of smoky breath in the auto light, this driver turning the pages over quite calm. And they were on to me all the time, O my brothers. Then Billyboy or

Dim. I couldn't say which one, said: 'About enough, droogie, I should think, shouldn't you?' Then they gave me one final tolchock on the litso each and I fell over and just laid there on the grass. It was cold but I was not feeling the cold. Then they dusted their rookers and put back on their shlems and tunics which they had taken off, and then they got back into the auto. 'Be viddying you some more sometime, Alex,' said Billyboy, and Dim just gave one of his old clowny guffs. The driver finished the page he was reading and put his book away, then he started the auto and they were off townwards, my ex-droog and ex-enemy waving. But I just laid there, fagged and shagged.

After a bit I was hurting bad, and then the rain started, all icy. I could viddy no lewdies in sight, nor no lights of houses. Where was I to go, who had no home and not much cutter in my carmans? I cried for myself boo hoo hoo. Then I got up and began walking.

# 4

Home, home, home, it was home I was wanting, and it was HOME I came to, brothers. I walked through the dark and followed not the town way but the way where the shoom of a like farm machine had been coming from. This brought me to a sort of village I felt I had viddied before, but was perhaps because all villages look the same, in the dark especially. Here were houses and there was a like drinking mesto, and right at the end of the village there was a malenky cottage on its oddy knocky, and I could viddy its name shining on the gate. HOME, it said. I was all dripping wet with this icy rain, so that my platties were no longer in the heighth of fashion but real miserable and like pathetic, and my luscious glory was a wet tangle cally mess all spread over my gulliver, and I was sure there were cuts and bruises all over my litso, and a couple of my zoobies sort of joggled loose when I touched them with my tongue or yahzick. And I was sore all over my plott and very thirsty, so that I kept opening my rot to the cold rain, and my stomach growled grrrrr all the time with not having had any pishcha since morning and then not very much, O my brothers.

HOME, it said, and perhaps here would be some veck to help. I opened the gate and sort of slithered down the path, the rain like turning to ice, and then I knocked gentle and pathetic on the door. No veck came, so I knocked a malenky bit longer and louder, and then I heard the shoom of nogas coming to the door. Then the door opened and a male goloss said: 'Yes, what is it?'

'Oh,' I said, 'please help. I've been beaten up by the police and just left to die on the road. Oh, please give me a drink of something and a sit by the fire, please, sir.'

The door opened full then, and I could viddy like warm light and a fire going crackle crackle within. 'Come in,' said this veck, 'whoever you are. God help you, you poor victim, come in and let's have a look at you.' So I like staggered in, and it was no big act I was putting on, brothers. I really felt done and finished. This kind veck put his rookers round my pletchoes and pulled me into this room where the fire was, and of course I knew right away now where it was and why HOME on the gate looked so familiar. I looked at this veck and he looked at me in a kind sort of way, and I remembered him well now. Of course he would not remember me, for in those carefree days I and my so-called droogs did all our bolshy dratsing and fillying and crasting in maskies which were real horrorshow disguises. He was a shortish veck in middle age, thirty, forty, fifty, and he had otchkies on. 'Sit down by the fire,' he said, 'and I'll get you some whisky and warm water. Dear dear dear, somebody *has* been beating you up.' And he gave a like tender look at my gulliver and litso.

'The police,' I said. 'The horrible ghastly police.'

'Another victim,' he said, like sighing. 'A victim of the modern age. I'll go and get you that whisky and then I must clean up your wounds a little.' And off he went. I had a look round this malenky comfortable room. It was nearly all books now and a fire and a couple of chairs, and you could viddy somehow that there wasn't a woman living there. On the table was a typewriter and a lot of like tumbled papers, and I remembered that this veck was a writer veck. *A Clockwork Orange*, that had been it. It was funny that that stuck in my mind. I must not let on, though, for I needed help and kindness now. Those horrible grahzny bratchnies in that terrible white mesto had done that to me, making me need help and kindness now and forcing me to want to give help and kindness myself, if anybody would take it.

'Here we are, then,' said this veck returning. He gave me this hot stimulating glassful to peet, and it made me feel better, and then he cleaned up these cuts on my litso. Then he said: 'You have a nice hot bath, I'll draw it for you, and then you can tell me all about it over a nice hot supper which I'll get ready while you're having the bath.' O my brothers, I could have wept at his kindness, and I think he must have viddied the old tears in my glazzies, for he said: 'There there there,' patting me on the pletcho.

Anyway, I went up and had this hot bath, and he brought in pyjamas and an over-gown for me to put on, all warmed by the fire, also a very worn pair of toofles. And now, brothers, though I was aching and full of pains all over, I felt I would soon feel a lot better. I ittied downstairs and viddied that in the kitchen he had set the table with knives and forks and a fine big loaf of kleb, also a bottle of PRIMA SAUCE, and soon he served out a nice fry of eggiwegs and lomticks of ham and bursting sausages and big bolshy mugs of hot sweet milky chai. It was nice sitting there in the warm, eating, and I found I was very hungry, so that after the fry I had to eat lomtick after lomtick of kleb and butter spread with strawberry jam out of a bolshy great pot. 'A lot better,' I said. 'How can I ever repay?'

'I think I know who you are,' he said. 'If you are who I think you are, then you've come, my friend, to the right place. Wasn't that your picture in the papers this morning? Are you the poor victim of this horrible new technique? If so, then you have been sent here by Providence. Tortured in prison, then thrown out to be tortured by the police. My heart goes out to you, poor poor boy.' Brothers, I could not get a slovo in, though I had my rot wide open to answer his questions. 'You are not the first to come here in distress,' he said. 'The police are fond of bringing their victims to the outskirts of this village. But it is providential that you, who are also another kind of victim, should come here. Perhaps, then, you have heard of me?'

I had to be very careful, brothers. I said: 'I have heard of *A Clockwork Orange*. I have not read it, but I have heard of it.'

'Ah,' he said, and his litso shone like the sun in its flaming morning glory. 'Now tell me about yourself.'

'Little enough to tell, sir,' I said, all humble. 'There was a foolish and boyish prank, my so-called friends persuading or rather forcing me to break into the house of an old ptitsa – lady, I mean. There was no real harm meant. Unfortunately the lady strained her good old heart in trying to throw me out, though I was quite ready to go of my own accord, and then she died. I was accused of being the cause of her death. So I was sent to prison, sir.'

'Yes yes yes, go on.'

'Then I was picked out by the Minister of the Inferior or Interior to have this Ludovico's veshch tried out on me.'

'Tell me all about it,' he said, leaning forward eager, his pullover elbows with all strawberry jam on them from the plate I'd pushed to one side. So I told him all about it. I told him the lot, all, my brothers. He was very eager to hear all, his glazzies like shining and his goobers apart, while the grease on the plates grew harder harder harder. When I had finished he got up from the table, nodding a lot and going hm hm hm, picking up the plates and other veshches from the table and taking them to the sink for washing up. I said:

'I will do that, sir, and gladly.'

'Rest, rest, poor lad,' he said, turning the tap on so that all steam came burping out. 'You've sinned, I suppose, but your punishment has been out of all proportion. They have turned you into something other than a human being. You have no power of choice any longer. You are committed to socially acceptable acts, a little machine capable only of good. And I see that clearly – that business about the marginal conditionings. Music and the sexual act, literature and art, all must be a source now not of pleasure but of pain.'

'That's right, sir,' I said, smoking one of this kind man's cork-tipped cancers.

'They always bite off too much,' he said, drying a plate like absent-mindedly. 'But the essential intention is the real sin. A man who cannot choose ceases to be a man.'

'That's what the charles said, sir,' I said. 'The prison chaplain, I mean.'

'Did he, did he? Of course he did. He'd have to, wouldn't he, being a Christian? Well, now then,' he said, still wiping the same plate he'd been wiping ten minutes ago, 'we shall have a few people in to see you tomorrow. I think you can be used, poor boy. I think that you can help dislodge this overbearing Government. To turn a decent young man into a piece of clockwork should not, surely, be seen as any triumph for any government, save one that boasts of its repressiveness.' He was still wiping this same plate. I said:

'Sir, you're still wiping that same plate, I agree with you, sir, about boasting. This Government seems to be very boastful.'

'Oh,' he said, like viddying this plate for the first time and then putting it down. 'I'm still not too handy,' he said, 'with domestic chores. My wife used to do them all and leave me to my writing.'

'Your wife, sir?' I said. 'Has she gone and left you?' I really wanted to know about his wife, remembering very well.

'Yes, left me,' he said, in a like loud and bitter goloss. 'She died, you see. She was brutally raped and beaten. The shock was very great. It was in this house,' his rookers were trembling, holding a wiping-up cloth, 'in that room next door. I have had to steel myself to continue to live here, but she would have wished me to stay where her fragrant memory still lingers. Yes yes yes. Poor little girl.' I viddied all clearly, my brothers, what had happened that far-off nochy, and viddying myself on that job, I began to feel I wanted to sick and the pain started up in my gulliver. This veck viddied this, because my litso felt it was all drained of red red krovvy, very pale, and he would be able to viddy this. 'You go to bed now,' he said kindly. 'I've got the spare room ready. Poor poor boy, you must have had a terrible time. A victim of the modern age, just as she was. Poor poor poor girl.'

# 5

I had a real horrorshow night's sleep, brothers, with no dreams at all, and the morning was very clear and like frosty, and there was the very pleasant like von of breakfast frying away down below. It took me some little time to remember where I was, as it always does, but it soon came back to me and then I felt like warmed and protected. But, as I laid there in the bed, waiting to be called down to breakfast, it struck me that I ought to get to know the name of this kind protecting and like motherly veck, so I had a pad round in my nagoy nogas looking for *A Clockwork Orange*, which would be bound to have his eemya in, he being the author. There was nothing in my bedroom except a bed and a chair and a light, so I ittied next door to this veck's own room, and there I viddied his wife on the wall, a bolshy blown-up photo, so I felt a malenky bit sick remembering. But there were two or three shelves of books there too, and there was, as I thought there must be, a copy of *A Clockwork Orange*, and on the back of the book, like on the spine, was the author's eemya – F. Alexander. Good Bog, I thought, he is another Alex. Then I leafed through, standing in his pyjamas and bare nogas but not feeling one malenky bit cold, the cottage being warm all through, and I could not viddy what the book was about. It seemed written in a very bezoomny like style, full of Ah and Oh and that cal, but what seemed to come out of it was that all lewdies nowadays were being turned into machines and that they were really – you and me and him and kiss-my-sharries – more like a natural growth like a fruit. F. Alexander seemed to think that we all like grow on what he called the world-tree in the world-orchard that like Bog or God planted, and we were there because Bog or God had need of us to quench his thirsty love, or some such cal. I didn't like the shoom of this at all, O my brothers, and wondered how bezoomny this F. Alexander really was, perhaps driven bezoomny by his wife's snuffing it. But then he called me down in a like sane veck's goloss, full of joy and love and all that cal, so down Your Humble Narrator went.

'You've slept long,' he said, ladling out boiled eggs and pulling black toast from under the grill. 'It's nearly ten already. I've been up hours, working.'

'Writing another book, sir?' I said.

'No no, not that now,' he said, and we sat down nice and droogy to the old crack crack crack of eggs and crackle crunch crunch of this black toast, very milky chai standing by in bolshy great morning mugs. 'No, I've been on the phone to various people.'

'I thought you didn't have a phone,' I said, spooning egg in and not watching out what I was saying.

'Why?' he said, very alert like some skorry animal with an egg-spoon in its rooker. 'Why shouldn't you think I have a phone?'

'Nothing,' I said, 'nothing, nothing.' And I wondered, brothers, how much he remembered of the earlier part of that distant nochy, me coming to the door with the old tale and saying to phone the doctor and she saying no phone. He took a very close smot at me but then went back to being like kind and cheerful and spooning up the old eggiweg. Munching away, he said:

'Yes, I've rung up various people who will be interested in your case. You can be a very potent weapon, you see, in ensuring that this present evil and wicked Government is not returned in the forthcoming election. The Government's big boast, you see, is the way it has dealt with crime these last months.' He looked at me very close again over his steaming egg, and I wondered again if he was viddying what part I had so far played in his jeezny. But he said: 'Recruiting brutal young roughs for the police. Proposing debilitating and will-sapping techniques of conditioning.' All these long slovos, brothers, and a like mad or bezoomny look in his glazzies. 'We've seen it all before,' he said, 'in other countries. The thin end of the wedge. Before we know where we are we shall have the full apparatus of totalitarianism.' 'Dear dear dear,' I thought, egging away and toast-crunching. I said:

'Where do I come into all this, sir?'

'You,' he said, still with this bezoomny look, 'are a living witness to these diabolical proposals. The people, the common people must know, must see.' He got up from his breakfast and started to walk up and down the kitchen, from the sink to the like larder, saying very gromky: 'Would they like their sons to become what you, poor victim, have become? Will not the Government itself now decide what is and what is not crime and pump out the life and guts and will of whoever sees fit to displease the Government?' He became quieter but did not go back to his egg. 'I've written an article,' he said, 'this morning, while you were sleeping. That will be out in a day or so, together with your unhappy picture. You shall sign it, poor boy, a record of what they have done to you.' I said:

'And what do you get out of all this, sir? I mean, besides the pretty polly you'll get for the article, as you call it? I mean, why are you so hot and strong against this Government, if I may make like so bold as to ask?'

He gripped the edge of the table and said, gritting his zoobies, which were very cally and all stained with cancer-smoke: 'Some of us have to fight. There are great traditions of liberty to defend. I am no partisan man. Where I see the infamy I seek to erase it. Party names mean nothing. The tradition of liberty means all. The common people will let it go, oh yes. They will sell liberty for a quieter life. That is why they must be prodded, *prodded* – ' And here, brothers, he picked up a fork and stuck it two or three razzes into the wall, so that it all got bent. Then he threw it on the floor. Very kindly he said: 'Eat well, poor boy, poor victim of the modern world,' and I could viddy quite clear he was going off his gulliver. 'Eat, eat. Eat my egg as well.' But I said:

'And what do I get out of this? Do I get cured of the way I am? Do I find myself able to slooshy the old Choral Symphony without being sick once more? Can I live like a normal jeezny again? What, sir, happens to me?'

He looked at me, brothers, as if he hadn't thought of that before and, anyway, it didn't matter compared with Liberty and all that cal, and he had a look of surprise at me saying what I said, as though I was being like selfish in wanting something for myself. Then he said: 'Oh, as I say, you're a living witness, poor boy. Eat up all your breakfast and then come and see what I've written, for it's going into *The Weekly Trumpet* under your name, you unfortunate victim.'

Well, brothers, what he had written was a very long and very weepy piece of writing, and as I read it I felt very sorry for the poor malchick who was govoreeting about his sufferings and how the Government had sapped his will and how it was up to all lewdies to not let such a rotten and evil Government rule them again, and then of course I realized that the poor suffering malchick was none other than YHN. 'Very good,' I said. 'Real horrorshow. Written well thou hast, O sir.' And then he looked at me very narrow and said:

'What?' It was like he had not slooshied me before.

'Oh, that,' I said, 'is what we call nadsat talk. All the teens use that, sir.' So then he ittied off to the kitchen to wash up the dishes, and I was left in these borrowed night platties and toofles, waiting to have done to me what was going to be done to me, because I had no plans for myself, O my brothers.

While the great F. Alexander was in the kitchen a dingalingaling came at the door. 'Ah,' he creeched, coming out wiping his rookers, 'it will be these people. I'll go.' So he went and let them in, a kind of rumbling hahaha of talk and hallo and filthy weather and how are things in the hallway, then they ittied into the room with the fire and the book and the article about how I had suffered, viddying me and going Aaaaah as they did it. There were three lewdies, and F. Alex gave me their eemyas. Z. Dolin was a very wheezy smoky kind of a veck, coughing kashl kashl kashl with the end of a cancer in his rot, spilling ash all down his platties and then brushing it away with like very impatient rookers. He was a malenky round veck, fat, with big thick-framed otchkies on. Then there was Something Something Rubinstein, a very tall and polite chelloveck with a real gentleman's goloss, very starry with a like eggy beard. And lastly there was D. B. da Silva who was like skorry in his movements and had this strong von of scent coming from him. They all had a real horrorshow look at me and seemed like overjoyed with what they viddied. Z. Dolin said:

'All right, all right, eh? What a superb device he can be, this boy. If anything, of course, he could for preference look even iller and more zombyish than he does. Anything for the cause. No doubt we can think of something.'

I did not like that crack about zombyish, brothers, and so I said: 'What goes on, bratties? What dost thou in mind for thy little droog have?' And then F. Alexander swooshed in with:

'Strange, strange, that manner of voice pricks me. We've come into contact before, I'm sure we have.' And he brooded, like frowning. I would have to watch this, O my brothers. D. B. da Silva said:

'Public meetings, mainly. To exhibit you at public meetings will be a tremendous help. And, of course, the newspaper angle is all tied up. A ruined life is the approach. We must inflame all hearts.' He showed his thirty-odd zoobies, very white against his dark-coloured litso, he looking a malenky bit like some foreigner. I said:

'Nobody will tell me what I get out of all this. Tortured in jail, thrown out of my home by my own parents and their filthy overbearing lodger, beaten by old men and near-killed by the millicents – what is to become of me?' The Rubinstein veck came in with:

'You will see, boy, that the Party will not be ungrateful. Oh, no. At the end of it all there will be some very acceptable little surprise for you. Just you wait and see.'

'There's only one veshch I require,' I creeched out, 'and that's to be normal and healthy as I was in the starry days, having my malenky bit of fun with *real* droogs and not those who just call themselves that and are really more like traitors. Can you do that, eh? Can any veck restore me to what I was? That's what I want and that's what I want to know.'

Kashl kashl kashl, coughed this Z. Dolin. 'A martyr to the cause of Liberty,' he said. 'You have your part to play and don't forget it. Meanwhile, we shall look after you.' And he began to stroke my left rooker as if I was like an idiot, grinning in a bezoomny way. I creeched:

'Stop treating me like a thing that's like got to be just used. I'm not an idiot you can impose on, you stupid bratchnies. Ordinary prestoopnicks are stupid, but I'm not ordinary and nor am I dim. Do you slooshy?'

'Dim,' said F. Alexander, like musing. 'Dim. That was a name somewhere, Dim.'

'Eh?' I said. 'What's Dim got to do with it? What do *you* know about Dim?' And then I said: 'Oh, Bog help us.' I didn't like the like look in F. Alexander's glazzies. I made for the door, wanting to go upstairs and get my platties and then itty off.

'I could almost believe,' said F. Alexander, showing his stained zoobies, his glazzies mad. 'But such things are impossible. For, by Christ, if he were I'd tear him. I'd split him, by God, yes yes, so I would.'

'There,' said D. B. da Silva, stroking his chest like he was a doggie to calm him down. 'It's all in the past. It was other people altogether.

We must help this poor victim. That's what we must do now, remembering the Future and our Cause.'

'I'll just get my platties,' I said, at the stair-foot, 'that is to say clothes, and then I'll be ittying off all on my oddy knocky. I mean, my gratitude for all, but I have my own jeezny to live.' Because, brothers, I wanted to get out of here real skorry. But Z. Dolin said:

'Ah, no. We have you, friend, and we keep you. You come with us. Everything will be all right, you'll see.' And he came up to me like to grab hold of my rooker again. Then, brothers, I thought of fight, but thinking of fight made me like want to collapse and sick, so I just stood. And then I saw this like madness in F. Alexander's glazzies and said:

'Whatever you say. I am in your rookers. But let's get it started and all over, brothers.' Because what I wanted now was to get out of this mesto called HOME. I was beginning not to like the like look of the glazzies of F. Alexander one malenky bit.

'Good,' said this Rubinstein. 'Get dressed and let's get started.'

'Dim dim dim,' F. Alexander kept saying in a like low mutter. 'What or who was this Dim?' I ittied upstairs real skorry and dressed in near two seconds flat. Then I was out with these three and into an auto, Rubinstein one side of me and Z. Dolin coughing kashl kashl kashl the other side, D. B. da Silva doing the driving, into the town and to a flatblock not really all that distant from what had used to be my own flatblock or home. 'Come, boy, out,' said Z. Dolin, coughing to make the cancer-end in his rot glow red like some malenky furnace. 'This is where you shall be installed.' So we ittied in, and there was like another of these Dignity of Labour veshches on the wall of the vestibule, and we upped in the lift, brothers, and then went into a flat like all the flats of all the flatblocks of the town. Very very malenky, with two bedrooms and one live-eat-work-room, the table of this all covered with books and papers and ink and bottles and all that cal. 'Here is your new home,' said D. B. da Silva. 'Settle here, boy. Food is in the food-cupboard. Pyjamas are in a drawer. Rest, rest, perturbed spirit.'

'Eh?' I said, not quite ponying that.

'All right,' said Rubinstein, with his starry goloss. 'We are now leaving you. Work has to be done. We'll be with you later. Occupy yourself as best you can.'

'One thing,' coughed Z. Dolin kashl kashl kashl. 'You saw what stirred in the tortured memory of our friend F. Alexander. Was it, by chance –? That is to say, did you –? I think you know what I mean. We won't let it go any further.'

'I've paid,' I said. 'Bog knows I've paid for what I did. I've paid not only like for myself but for those bratchnies too that called themselves my droogs.' I felt violent so then I felt a bit sick. 'I'll lay down a bit,' I said. 'I've been through terrible terrible times.'

'You have,' said D. B. da Silva, showing all his thirty zoobies. 'You do that.'

So they left me, brothers. They ittied off about their business, which I took to be about politics and all that cal, and I was on the bed, all on my oddy knocky with everything very very quiet. I just laid there with my sabogs kicked off my nogas and my tie loose, like all bewildered and not knowing what sort of a jeezny I was going to live now. And all sorts of like pictures kept like passing through my gulliver, of the different chellovecks I'd met at school and in the Staja, and the different veshches that had happened to me, and how there was not one veck you could trust in the whole bolshy world. And then I like dozed off, brothers.

When I woke up I could hear slooshy music coming out of the wall, real gromky, and it was that that had dragged me out of my bit of like sleep. It was a symphony that I knew real horrorshow but had not slooshied for many a year, namely the Symphony Number Three of the Danish veck Otto Skadelig, a very gromky and violent piece, especially in the first movement, which was what was playing now. I slooshied for two seconds in like interest and joy, but then it all came over me, the start of the pain and the sickness, and I began to groan deep down in my keeshkas. And then there I was, me who had loved music so much, crawling off the bed and going oh oh oh to myself, and then bang bang banging on the wall creeching: 'Stop, stop it, turn it off!' But it went on and it seemed to be like louder. So I crashed at the wall till my knuckles were all red red krovvy and torn skin, creeching and creeching, but the music did not stop. Then I thought

I had to get away from it, so I lurched out of the malenky bedroom and ittied skorry to the front door of the flat, but this had been locked from the outside and I could not get out. And all the time the music got more and more gromky, like it was all a deliberate torture, O my brothers. So I stuck my little fingers real deep in my ookos, but the trombones and kettledrums blasted through gromky enough. So I creeched again for them to stop and went hammer hammer hammer on the wall, but it made not one malenky bit of difference. 'Oh, what am I to do?' I boohooed to myself. 'Oh, Bog in Heaven help me.' I was like wandering all over the flat in pain and sickness, trying to shut out the music and like groaning deep out of my guts, and then on top of the pile of books and papers and all that cal that was on the table in the living-room I viddied what I had to do and what I had wanted to do until those old men in the Public Biblio and then Dim and Billyboy disguised as rozzes stopped me, and that was to do myself in, to snuff it, to blast off for ever out of this wicked and cruel world. What I viddied was the slovo DEATH on the cover of a like pamphlet, even though it was only DEATH to THE GOVERNMENT. And like it was Fate there was another malenky booklet which had an open window on the cover, and it said: 'Open the window to fresh air, fresh ideas, a new way of living.' And so I knew that was like telling me to finish it all off by jumping out. One moment of pain, perhaps, and then sleep for ever and ever and ever.

The music was still pouring in all brass and drums and the violins miles up through the wall. The window in the room where I had laid down was open. I ittied to it and viddied a fair drop to the autos and buses and walking chellovecks below. I creeched out to the world: 'Good-bye, good-bye, may Bog forgive you for a ruined life.' Then I got on to the sill, the music blasting away to my left, and I shut my glazzies and felt the cold wind on my litso, then I jumped.

# 6

I jumped, O my brothers, and I fell on the sidewalk hard, but I did not snuff it, oh no. If I had snuffed it I would not be here to write what I written have. It seems that the jump was not from a big enough heighth to kill. But I cracked my back and my wrists and nogas and felt very bolshy pain before I passed out, brothers, with astonished and surprised litsos of chellovecks in the streets looking at me from above. And just before I passed out I viddied clear that not one chelloveck in the whole horrid world was for me and that that music through the wall had all been like arranged by those who were supposed to be my like new droogs and that it was some veshch like this that they wanted for their horrible selfish and boastful politics. All that was in like a million millionth part of one minoota before I threw over the world and the sky and the litsos of the staring chellovecks that were above me.

Where I was when I came back to jeezny after a long black black gap of it might have been a million years was a hospital, all white and with this von of hospitals you get, all like sour and smug and clean. These antiseptic veshches you get in hospitals should have a real horrorshow von of like frying onions or of flowers. I came very slow back to knowing who I was and I was all bound up in white and I could not feel anything in my plott, pain nor sensation nor any veshch at all. All round my gulliver was a bandage and there were bits of stuff like stuck to my litso, and my rookers were all in bandages and like bits of stick were like fixed to my fingers like on it might be flowers to make them grow straight, and my poor old nogas were all straightened out too, and it was all bandages and wire cages and into my right rooker, near the pletcho, was red red krovvy dripping from a jar upside down. But I could not feel anything, O my brothers. There was a nurse sitting by my bed and she was reading some book that was all very dim print and you could viddy it was a story because of a lot of inverted commas, and she was like breathing hard uh uh uh over it, so it must have been a story about the old in-out in-out. She was a real horrorshow devotchka, this nurse, with a very red rot and like long lashes over her glazzies, and under her like very stiff uniform you could viddy she had very horrorshow groodies. So I said to her: 'What gives, O my little sister? Come thou and have a nice lay-down with your malenky droog in this bed.' But the slovos didn't come out horrorshow at all, it being as though my rot was all stiffened up, and I could feel with my yahzick that some of my zoobies were no longer there. But this nurse like jumped and dropped her book on the floor and said:

'Oh, you've recovered consciousness.'

That was like a big rotful for a malenky ptitsa like her, and I tried to say so, but the slovos came out only like er er er. She ittied off and left me on my oddy knocky, and I could viddy now that I was in a malenky room of my own, not in one of these long wards like I had been in as a very little malchick, full of coughing dying starry vecks all around to make you want to get well and fit again. It had been like diphtheria I had had then, O my brothers.

It was like now as though I could not hold to being conscious all that long, because I was like asleep again almost right away, very skorry, but in a minoota or two I was sure that this nurse ptitsa had come back and had brought chellovecks in white coats with her and they were viddying me very frowning and going hm hm hm at Your Humble Narrator. And with them I was sure there was the old charles from the Staja govoreeting: 'Oh my son, my son,' breathing a like very stale von of whisky on to me and then saying: 'But I would not stay, oh no. I could not in no wise subscribe to what those bratchnies are going to do to other poor prestoopnicks. So I got out and am preaching sermons now about it all, my little beloved son in J.C.'

I woke up again later on and who should I viddy there round the bed but the three from whose flat I had jumped out, namely D. B. da Silva and Something Something Rubinstein and Z. Dolin. 'Friend,' one of these vecks was saying, but I could not viddy, or slooshy horrorshow which one, 'friend, little friend,' this goloss was saying, 'the people are on fire with indignation. You have killed those horrible boastful villains' chances of re-election. They will go and will go for ever and ever. You have served Liberty well.' I tried to say:

'If I had died it would have been even better for you political bratchnies, would it not, pretending and treacherous droogs as you are.' But all that came out was er er er. Then one of these three seemed to hold out a lot of bits cut from gazettas and what I could viddy was a horrible picture of me all krovvy on a stretcher being carried off and I seemed to like remember a kind of a popping of lights which must have been photographer vecks. Out of one glazz I could read like headlines which were sort of trembling in the rooker of the chelloveck that held them, like BOY VICTIM OF CRIMINAL REFORM SCHEME and GOVERNMENT AS MURDERER and then there was like a picture of a veck that looked familiar to me and it said OUT OUT OUT, and that would be the Minister of the Inferior or Interior. Then the nurse ptitsa said:

'You shouldn't be exciting him like that. You shouldn't be doing anything that will make him upset. Now come on, let's have you out.' I tried to say:

'Out out out,' but it was er er er again. Anyway, these three political vecks went. And I went, too, only back to the land, back to all blackness lit up by like odd dreams which I didn't know whether they were dreams or not, O my brothers. Like for instance I had this idea of my whole plott or body being like emptied of as it might be dirty water and then filled up again with clean. And then there were really lovely and horrorshow dreams of being in some veck's auto that had been crasted by me and driving up and down the world all on my oddy knocky running lewdies down and hearing them creech they were dying, and in me no pain and no sickness. And also there were dreams of doing the old in-out in-out with devotchkas, forcing like them down on the ground and making them have it and everybody standing round claping their rookers and cheering like bezoomny. And then I woke up again and it was my pee and em come to viddy their ill son, my em boohooing real horrorshow. I could govoreet a lot better now and could say:

'Well well well well well, what gives? What makes you think you are like welcome?' My papapa said, in a like ashamed way:

'You were in the papers, son. It said they had done great wrong to you. It said how the Government drove you to try and do yourself in. And it was our fault too, in a way, son. Your home's your home, when all's said and done, son.' And my mum kept on going boohoohoo and looking ugly as kiss-my-sharries. So I said:

'And how beeth thy new son Joe? Well and healthy and prosperous, I trust and pray.' My mum said:

'Oh, Alex Alex. Owwwwwwwww.' My papapa said:

'A very awkward thing, son. He got into a bit of trouble with the police and was done by the police.'

'Really?' I said. 'Really? Such a good sort of chelloveck and all. Amazed proper I am, honest.'

'Minding his own business he was,' said my pee. 'And the police told him to move on. Waiting at a corner he was, son, to see a girl he was going to meet. And they told him to move on and he said he had rights like everybody else, and then they sort of fell on top of him and hit him about cruel.'

'Terrible,' I said. 'Really terrible. And where is the poor boy now?'

'Owwwww,' boohooed my mum. 'Gone back owwwwwwme.'

'Yes,' said dad. 'He's gone back to his own home town to get better. They've had to give his job here to somebody else.'

'So now,' I said, 'you're willing for me to move back in again and things be like they were before.'

'Yes, son,' said my papapa. 'Please, son.'

'I'll consider it,' I said. 'I'll think about it real careful.'

'Owwwww,' went my mum.

'Ah, shut it,' I said, 'or I'll give you something proper to yowl and creech about. Kick your zoobies in I will.' And, O my brothers, saying that made me feel a malenky bit better, as if all like fresh red red krovvy was flowing all through my plott. That was something I had to think about. It was like as though to get better I had had to get worse.

'That's no way to speak to your mother, son,' said my papapa. 'After all, she brought you into the world.'

'Yes,' I said, 'And a right grahzny vonny world too.' I shut my glazzies tight in like pain and said: 'Go away now. I'll think about coming back. But things will have to be very different.'

'Yes, son,' said my pee. 'Anything you say.'

'You'll have to make up your mind,' I said, 'who's to be boss.'

'Owwwwww,' my mum went on.

'Very good, son,' said my papapa. 'Things will be as you like. Only get well.'

When they had gone I laid and thought a bit about different veshches, like all different pictures passing through my gulliver, and when the nurse ptitsa came back in and like straightened the sheets on the bed I said to her:

'How long is it I've been in here?'

'A week or so,' she said.

'And what have they been doing to me?'

'Well,' she said, 'you were all broken up and bruised and had sustained severe concussion and had lost a lot of blood. They've had to put all that right, haven't they?'

'But,' I said, 'has anyone been doing anything with my gulliver? What I mean is, have they been playing around with inside like my brain?'

'Whatever they've done,' she said, 'it'll all be for the best.'

But a couple of days later a couple of like doctor vecks came in, both youngish vecks with these very sladky smiles, and they had like a picture book with them. One of them said: 'We want you to have a look at these and to tell us what you think about them. All right?'

'What giveth, O little droogies?' I said. 'What new bezoomny idea dost thou in mind have?' So they both had a like embarrassed smeck at that and then they sat down either side of the bed and opened up this book. On the first page there was like a photograph of a bird-nest full of eggs.

'Yes?' one of these doctor vecks said.

'A bird-nest,' I said, 'full of like eggs. Very very nice.'

'And what would you like to do about it?' the other one said.

'Oh,' I said, 'smash them. Pick up the lot and like throw them against a wall or a cliff or something and then viddy them all smash up real horrorshow.'

'Good good,' they both said, and then the page was turned. It was like a picture of one of these bolshy great birds called peacocks with all its tail spread out in all colours in a very boastful way. 'Yes?' said one of these vecks.

'I would like,' I said, 'to pull out like all those feathers in its tail and slooshy it creech blue murder. For being so like boastful.'

'Good,' they both said, 'good good good.' And they went on turning the pages. There were like pictures of real horrorshow devotchkas, and I said I would like to give them the old in-out in-out with lots of ultra-violence. There were like pictures of chellovecks being given the boot straight in the litso and all red red krovvy everywhere and I said I would like to be in on that. And there was a picture of the old nagoy droog of the prison charlie's carrying his cross up a hill, and I said I would like to have the old hammer and nails. Good good good, I said:

'What is all this?'

'Deep hypnopaedia,' or some such slovo, said one of these two vecks. 'You seem to be cured.'

'Cured?' I said. 'Me tied down to this bed like this and you say cured? Kiss my sharries is what I say.'

'Wait,' the other said. 'It won't be long now.'

So I waited and, O my brothers, I got a lot better, munching away at eggiwegs and lomticks of toast and peeting bolshy great mugs of milky chai, and then one day they said I was going to have a very very very special visitor.

'Who?' I said, while they straightened the bed and combed my luscious glory for me, me having the bandage off now from my gulliver and the hair growing again.

'You'll see, you'll see,' they said. And I viddied all right. At two-thirty of the afternoon there were like all photographers and men from gazettas with notebooks and pencils and all that cal. And, brothers, they near trumpeted a bolshy fanfare for this great and important veck who was coming to viddy Your Humble Narrator. And in he came, and of course it was none other than the Minister of the Interior or Inferior, dressed in the heighth of fashion and with this very upperclass haw haw haw goloss. Flash flash bang went the cameras when he put out his rooker to me to shake it. I said:

'Well well well well well. What giveth then, old droogie?' Nobody seemed to quite pony that, but somebody said in a like harsh goloss:

'Be more respectful, boy, in addressing the Minister.'

'Yarbles,' I said, like snarling like a doggie. 'Bolshy great yarblockos to thee and thine.'

'All right, all right,' said the Interior Inferior one very skorry. 'He speaks to me as a friend, don't you, son?'

'I am everyone's friend,' I said. 'Except to my enemies.'

'And who are your enemies?' said the Minister, while all the gazetta vecks went scribble scribble scribble. 'Tell us that, my boy.'

'All who do me wrong,' I said, 'are my enemies.'

'Well,' said the Int Inf Min, sitting down by my bed. 'I and the Government of which I am a member want you to regard us as friends. Yes, friends. We have put you right, yes? You are getting the best of treatment. We never wished you harm, but there are some who did and do. And I think you know who those are.'

'Yes yes yes,' he said. 'There are certain men who wanted to use you, yes, use you for political ends. They would have been glad, yes, glad for you to be dead, for they thought they could then blame it all on the Government. I think you know who those men are.'

'There is a man,' said the Intinfmin, 'called F. Alexander, a writer of subversive literature, who has been howling for your blood. He has been mad with desire to stick a knife in you. But you're safe from him now. We put him away.'

'He was supposed to be like a droogie,' I said. 'Like a mother to me was what he was.'

'He found out that you had done wrong to him. At least,' said the Min very very skorry, 'he believed you had done wrong. He formed this idea in his mind that you had been responsible for the death of someone near and dear to him.'

'What you mean,' I said, 'is that he was told.'

'He had this idea,' said the Min. 'He was a menace. We put him away for his own protection. And also,' he said, 'for yours.'

'Kind,' I said. 'Most kind of thou.'

'When you leave here,' said the Min, 'you will have no worries. We shall see to everything. A good job on a good salary. Because you are helping us.'

'Am I?' I said.

'We always help our friends, don't we?' And then he took my rooker and some veck creeched: 'Smile!' and I smiled like bezoomny without thinking, and then flash flash crack flash bang there were pictures being taken of me and the Intinfmin all droogy together. 'Good boy,' said this great chelloveck. 'Good good boy. And now, see, a present.'

What was brought in now, brothers, was a big shiny box, and I viddied clear what sort of a veshch it was. It was a stereo. It was put down next to the bed and opened up and some veck plugged its lead into the wall-socket. 'What shall it be?' asked a veck with otchkies on his nose, and he had in his rookers lovely shiny sleeves full of music. 'Mozart? Beethoven? Schoenberg? Carl Orff?'

'The Ninth,' I said. 'The glorious Ninth.'

And the Ninth it was, O my brothers. Everybody began to leave nice and quiet while I laid there with my glazzies closed, slooshying the lovely music. The Min said: 'Good good boy,' patting me on the pletcho, then he ittied off. Only one veck was left, saying: 'Sign here, please.' I opened my glazzies up to sign, not knowing what I was signing and not, O my brothers, caring either. Then I was left alone with the glorious Ninth of Ludwig van.

Oh, it was gorgeosity and yumyumyum. When it came to the Scherzo I could viddy myself very clear running and running on like very light and mysterious nogas, carving the whole litso of the creeching world with my cut-throat britva. And there was the slow movement and the lovely last singing movement still to come. I was cured all right.

# 7

'What's it going to be then, eh?'

There was me, Your Humble Narrator, and my three droogs, that is Len, Rick, and Bully, Bully being called Bully because of his bolshy big neck and very gromky goloss which was just like some bolshy great bull bellowing auuuuuuuh. We were sitting in the Korova Milkbar making up our rassoodocks what to do with the evening, a flip dark chill winter bastard though dry. All round were chellovecks well away on milk plus vellocet and synthemesc and drencrom and other veshches which take you far far far away from this wicked and real world into the land to viddy Bog And All His Holy Angels And Saints in your left sabog with lights bursting and spurting all over your mozg. What we were peeting was the old moloko with knives in it, as we used to say, to sharpen you up and make you ready for a bit of dirty twenty-to-one, but I've told you all that before.

We were dressed in the heighth of fashion, which in those days was these very wide trousers and a very loose black shiny leather like jerkin over an open-necked shirt with a like scarf tucked in. At this time too it was the heighth of fashion to use the old britva on the gulliver, so that most of the gulliver was like bald and there was hair only on the sides. But it was always the same on the old nogas – real horrorshow bolshy big boots for kicking litsos in.

'What's it going to be then, eh?'

I was like the oldest of we four, and they all looked up to me as their leader, but I got the idea sometimes that Bully had the thought in his gulliver that he would like to take over, this being because of his bigness and the gromky goloss that bellowed out of him when he was on the warpath. But all the ideas came from Your Humble, O my brothers, and also there was this veshch that I had been famous and had had my picture and articles and all that cal in the gazettas. Also I had by far the best job of all we four, being in the National Gramodisc Archives on the music side with a real horrorshow carman full of pretty polly at the week's end and a lot of nice free discs for my own malenky self on the side.

This evening in the Korova there was a fair number of vecks and ptitsas and devotchkas and malchicks smecking and peeting away, and cutting through their govoreeting and the burbling of the in-the-landers with their 'Gorgor fallatuke and the worm sprays in filltip slaughterballs' and all that cal you could slooshy a popdisc on the stereo, this being Ned Achimota singing 'That Day, Yeah, That Day'. At the counter were three devotchkas dressed in the heighth of nadsat fashion, that is to say long uncombed hair dyed white and false groodies sticking out a metre or more and very very tight short skirts with all like frothy white underneath, and Bully kept saying: 'Hey, get in there we could, three of us. Old Len is not interested. Leave old

Len alone with his God.' And Len kept saying: 'Yarbles yarbles. Where is the spirit of all for one and one for all, eh boy?' Suddenly I felt both very very tired and also full of tingly energy, and I said:

'Out out out out out.'

'Where to?' said Rick, who had a litso like a frog's.

'Oh, just to viddy what's doing in the great outside,' I said. But somehow, my brothers, I felt very bored and a bit hopeless, and I had been feeling that a lot these days. So I turned to the chelloveck nearest me on the big plush seat that ran right round the whole mesto, a chelloveck, that is, who was burbling away under the influence, and I fisted him real skorry ack ack ack in the belly. But he felt it not, brothers, only burbling away with his 'Cart cart virtue, where in toptails lieth the pop-poppicorns?' So we scatted out into the big winter nochy.

We walked down Marghanita Boulevard and there were no milli-cents patrolling that way, so when we met a starry veck coming away from a news-kiosk where he had been kupetting a gazetta I said to Bully: 'All right, Bully boy, thou canst if thou like wishest.' More and more these days I had been just giving the orders and standing back to viddy them being carried out. So Bully cracked into him er er er, and the other two tripped him and kicked at him, smecking away, while he was down and then let him crawl off to where he lived, like whimpering to himself. Bully said:

'How about a nice yummy glass of something to keep out the cold, O Alex?' For we were not too far from the Duke of New York. The other two nodded yes yes yes but all looked at me to viddy whether that was all right. I nodded too and so off we ittied. Inside the snug there were these starry ptitsas or sharps or baboochkas you will remember from the beginning and they all started on their: 'Evening, lads, God bless you, boys, best lads living, that's what you are,' waiting for us to say: 'What's it going to be, girls?' Bully rang the collocoll and a waiter came in rubbing his rookers on his grazzy apron. 'Cutter on the table, droogies,' said Bully, pulling out his own rattling and chinking mound of deng. 'Scotchmen for us and the same for the old baboochkas, eh?' And then I said:

'Ah, to hell. Let them buy their own.' I didn't know what it was, but these last days I had become like mean. There had come into my gulliver a like desire to keep all my pretty polly to myself, to like hoard it all up for some reason. Bully said:

'What gives, bratty? What's coming over old Alex?'

'Ah, to hell,' I said. 'I don't know. I don't know. What it is is I don't like just throwing away my hard-earned pretty polly, that's what it is.'

'Earned?' said Rick. 'Earned? It doesn't have to be earned, as well thou knowest, old droogie. Took, that's all, just took, like.' And he smecked real gromky and I viddied one or two of his zoobies weren't all that horrorshow.

'Ah,' I said, 'I've got some thinking to do.' But viddying these baboochkas looking all eager like for some free alc, I like shrugged my pletchoes and pulled out my own cutter from my trouser carman, notes and coin all mixed together, and plonked it tinkle crackle on the table.

'Scotchmen all round, right,' said the waiter. But for some reason I said:

'No, boy, for me make it one small beer, right.' Len said:

'This I do not much go for,' and he began to put his rooker on my gulliver, like kidding I must have fever, but I like snarled doggy-wise for him to give over skorry. 'All right, all right, droog,' he said. 'As thou like sayest.' But Bully was having a smot with his rot open at something that had come out of my carman with the pretty polly I'd put on the table. He said:

'Well well well. And we never knew.'

'Give me that,' I snarled and grabbed it skorry. I couldn't explain how it had got there, brothers, but it was a photograph I had scissored out of the old gazetta and it was of a baby. It was of a baby gurgling goo goo goo with all like moloko dribbling from its rot and looking up and like smecking at everybody, and it was all nagoy and its flesh was like in all folds with being a very fat baby. There was then like a bit of haw haw haw struggling to get hold of this bit of paper from me, so I had to snarl again at them and I grabbed the photo and tore it up into tiny teeny pieces and let it fall like a bit of snow on to the floor. The whisky came in then and the starry baboochkas said: 'Good health, lads, God bless you, boys, the best lads living, that's what you are,' and all that cal. And one of them who was all lines and wrinkles and no zoobies in her shrunken old rot said: 'Don't tear up money, son. If you don't need it give it them as does,' which was very bold and forward of her. But Rick said:

'Money that was not, O baboochka. It was a picture of a dear little itsy witsy bitsy bit of a baby.' I said:

'I'm getting just that bit tired, that I am. It's you who's the babies, you lot. Scoffing and grinning and all you can do is smeck and give people bolshy cowardly tolchocks when they can't give them back.' Bully said:

'Well now, we always thought it was you who was the king of that and also the teacher. Not well, that's the trouble with thou, old droogie.'

I viddied this sloppy glass of beer I had on the table in front of me and felt like all vomity within, so I went 'Aaaaah' and poured all the frothy vonny cal all over the floor. One of the starry ptitsas said:

'Waste not want not.' I said:

'Look, droogies. Listen. Tonight I am somehow just not in the mood. I know not why or how it is, but there it is. You three go your own ways this nightwise, leaving me out. Tomorrow we shall meet same place same time, me hoping to be like a lot better.'

'Oh,' said Bully, 'right sorry I am.' But you could viddy a like gleam in his glazzies, because now he would be taking over for this nochy. Power power, everybody like wants power. 'We can postpone till tomorrow,' said Bully, 'what we in mind had. Namely, that bit of shop-crasting in Gagarin Street. Flip horror-show takings there, droog, for the having.'

'No,' I said. 'You postpone nothing. You just carry on in your own like style. Now,' I said, 'I itty off.' And I got up from my chair.

'Where to, then?' asked Rick.

'That know I not,' I said. 'Just to be on like my own and sort things out.' You could viddy the old baboochkas were real puzzled at me going out like that and like all morose and not the bright and smecking malchickiwick you will remember. But I said: 'Ah, to hell, to hell,' and scatted out all on my oddy knocky into the street.

It was dark and there was a wind sharp as a nozh getting up, and there were very very few lewdies about. There were these patrol cars with brutal rozzes inside them like cruising about, and now and then on the corner you would viddy a couple of very young millicents stamping against the bitchy cold and letting out steam breath on the winter air, O my brothers. I suppose really a lot of the old ultra-violence and crasting was dying out now, the rozzes being so brutal with who they caught, though it had become like a fight between naughty nadsats and the rozzes who could be more skorry with the nozh and the britva and the stick and even the gun. But what was the matter with me these days was that I didn't like care much. It was like something soft getting into me and I could not pony why. What I wanted these days I did not know. Even the music I liked to slooshy in my own malenky den was what I would have smecked at before, brothers. I was slooshying more like malenky romantic songs, what they call *Lieder*, just a goloss and a piano, very quiet and like yearny, different from when it had been all bolshy orchestras and me lying on the bed between the violins and the trombones and kettledrums. There was something happening inside me, and I wondered if it was like some disease or if it was what they had done to me that time upsetting my gulliver and perhaps going to make me real bezoomny.

So thinking like this with my gulliver bent and my rookers stuck in my trouser carmans I walked the town, brothers, and at last I began to feel very tired and also in great need of a nice bolshy chasha of milky chai. Thinking about this chai, I got a sudden like picture of me sitting before a bolshy fire in an armchair peeting away at this chai, and what was funny and very very strange was that I seemed to have turned into a very starry chelloveck, about seventy years old, because I could viddy my own voloss, which was very grey, and I also had whiskers, and these were very grey too. I could viddy myself as an old man, sitting by a fire, and then the like picture vanished. But it was very like strange.

I came to one of these tea-and-coffee mestos, brothers, and I could viddy through the long long window that it was full of very dull lewdies, like ordinary, who had these very patient and expressionless litsos and would do no harm to no one, all sitting there and govoreeting like quietly and peeting away at their nice harmless chai and coffee. I ittied inside and went up to the counter and bought me a nice hot chai with plenty of moloko, then I ittied to one of these tables and sat down to peet it. There was a like young couple at this table, peeting and smoking filter-tip cancers, and govoreeting and smecking very quietly between themselves, but I took no notice of them and just went on peeting away and like dreaming and wondering what it was in me that was like changing and what was going to happen to me. But I viddied that the devotchka at this table who was with this chelloveck was real horrorshow, not the sort you would want to like throw down and give the old in-out in-out to, but with a horrorshow plott and litso and a smiling rot and very very fair voloss and all that cal. And then the veck with her, who had a hat on his gulliver and had his litso like turned away from me, swivelled round to viddy the bolshy big clock they had on the wall in this mesto, and then I viddied who he was and then he viddied who I was. It was Pete, one of my three droogs from those days when it was Georgie and Dim and him and me. It was Pete like looking a lot older though he could not now be more than nineteen and a bit, and he had a bit of a moustache and an ordinary day-suit and this hat on. I said:

'Well well well, droogie, what gives? Very very long time no viddy.' He said:

'It's little Alex, isn't it?'

'None other,' I said. 'A long long long time since those dead and gone good days. And now poor Georgie, they told me, is underground and old Dim is a brutal millicent, and here is thou and here is I, and what news hast thou, old droogie?'

'He talks funny, doesn't he?' said this devotchka, like giggling.

'This,' said Pete to the devotchka, 'is an old friend. His name is Alex. May I,' he said to me, 'introduce my wife?'

My rot fell wide open then. 'Wife?' I like gaped. 'Wife wife wife? Ah no, that cannot be. Too young art thou to be married, old droog. Impossible impossible.'

This devotchka who was like Pete's wife (impossible impossible) giggled again and said to Pete: 'Did you used to talk like that too?'

'Well,' said Pete, and he like smiled. 'I'm nearly twenty. Old enough to be hitched, and it's been two months already. You were very young and very forward, remember.'

'Well,' I like gaped still. 'Over this get can I not, old droogie. Pete married. Well well well.'

'We have a small flat,' said Pete. 'I am earning very small money at State Marine Insurance, but things will get better, that I know. And Georgina here –'

'What again is that name?' I said, rot still open like bezoomny. Pete's wife (wife, brothers) like giggled again.

'Georgina,' said Pete. 'Georgina works too. Typing, you know. We manage, we manage.' I could not, brothers, take my glazzies off him, really. He was like grown up now, with a grown-up goloss and all. 'You must,' said Pete, 'come and see us sometime. You still,' he said, 'look very young, despite all your terrible experiences. Yes yes yes, we've read all about them. But, of course, you *are* very young still.'

'Eighteen,' I said, 'Just gone.'

'Eighteen, eh?' said Pete. 'As old as that. Well well well. Now,' he said, 'we have to be going.' And he like gave this Georgina of his a like loving look and pressed one of her rookers between his and she gave him one of these looks back, O my brothers. 'Yes,' said Pete, turning back to me, 'we're off to a little party at Greg's.'

'Greg?' I said.

'Oh, of course,' said Pete, 'you wouldn't know Greg, would you? Greg is after your time. While you were away Greg came into the picture. He runs little parties, you know. Mostly wine-cup and word-games. But very nice, very pleasant, you know. Harmless, if you see what I mean.'

'Yes,' I said. 'Harmless. Yes, yes, I viddy that real horror-show.' And this Georgina devotchka giggled again at my slovos. And then these two ittied off to their vonny word-games at this Greg's, whoever he was. I was left all on my oddy knocky with my milky chai, which was getting cold now, like thinking and wondering.

Perhaps that was it, I kept thinking. Perhaps I was getting too old for the sort of jeezny I had been leading, brothers. I was eighteen now, just gone. Eighteen was not a young age. At eighteen old Wolfgang Amadeus had written concertos and symphonies and operas and oratorios and all that cal, no, not cal, heavenly music. And then there was old Felix M. with his *Midsummer Night's Dream* Overture. And there were others. And there was this like French poet set by old Benjy Britt, who had done all his best poetry by the age of fifteen, O my brothers. Arthur, his first name. Eighteen was not all that young an age, then. But what was I going to do?

Walking the dark chill bastards of winter streets after ittying off from this chai and coffee mesto, I kept viddying like visions, like these cartoons in the gazettas. There was Your Humble Narrator Alex coming home from work to a good hot plate of dinner, and there was this ptitsa all welcoming and greeting like loving. But I could not viddy her all that horrorshow, brothers, I could not think who it might be. But I had this sudden very strong idea that if I walked into the room next to this room where the fire was burning away and my hot dinner laid on the table, there I should find what I really wanted, and now it all tied up, that picture scissored out of the gazetta and meeting old Pete like that. For in that other room in a cot was laying gurgling goo goo goo my son. Yes yes yes, brothers, my son. And now I felt this bolshy big hollow inside my plott, feeling very surprised too at myself. I knew what was happening, O my brothers. I was like growing up.

Yes yes yes, there it was. Youth must go, ah yes. But youth is only being in a way like it might be an animal. No, it is not just like being an animal so much as being like one of these malenky toys you viddy being sold in the streets, like little chellovecks made out of tin and with a spring inside and then a winding handle on the outside and you wind it up grrr grrr grrr and off it itties, like walking, O my brothers. But it itties in a straight line and bangs straight into things bang bang and it cannot help what it is doing. Being young is like being like one of these malenky machines.

My son, my son. When I had my son I would explain all that to him when he was starry enough to like understand. But then I knew he would not understand or would not want to understand at all and would do all the veshches I had done, yes perhaps even killing some poor starry forella surrounded with mewing kots and koshkas, and I would not be able to really stop him. And nor would he be able to stop his own son, brothers. And so it would itty on to like the end of the world, round and round and round, like some bolshy gigantic like chelloveck, like old Bog Himself (by courtesy of Korova Milk-bar) turning and turning and turning a vonny grahzny orange in his gigantic rookers.

But first of all, brothers, there was this veshch of finding some devotchka or other who would be a mother to this son. I would have to start on that tomorrow, I kept thinking. That was something like new to do. That was something I would have to get started on, a new like chapter beginning.

That's what it's going to be then, brothers, as I come to the like end of this tale. You have been everywhere with your little droog Alex, suffering with him, and you have viddied some of the most grahzny bratchnies old Bog ever made, all on to your old droog Alex. And all it was was that I was young. But now as I end this story, brothers, I am not young, not no longer, oh no. Alex like groweth up, oh yes.

But where I itty now, O my brothers, is all on my oddy knocky, where you cannot go. Tomorrow is all like sweet flowers and the turning vonny earth and the stars and the old Luna up there and your old droog Alex all on his oddy knocky seeking like a mate. And all that cal. A terrible grahzny vonny world, really, O my brothers. And so farewell from your little droog. And to all others in this story profound shooms of lip-music brrrrrr. And they can kiss my sharries. But you, O my brothers, remember sometimes thy little Alex that was. Amen. And all that cal.

# PENGUIN MODERN CLASSICS

---

**THE MONKEY WRENCH GANG**
EDWARD ABBEY

'A man of great passion and love of the natural order' Robert Redford

The construction of the colossal Glen Canyon Dam on the Colorado River spurs an oddball quartet of eco-activists to join forces in a noble cause. A Vietnam veteran who loves booze, guns and the great outdoors, a billboard-burning doctor, a feminist revolutionary and a polygamist riverboat guide – the Monkey Wrench Gang go up against the vultures of big business to sabotage the strip mines, power plants and concrete dams that are destroying vast tracts of the wilderness, through peaceful means – or otherwise …

Scandalizing the establishment and read by others as a call-to-arms when it appeared in 1975, *The Monkey Wrench Gang* is a wildly funny and provocatively satirical book that ignited the flames of environmental activism.

'A terrific read – funny, perceptive, brutally honest, and extremely timely'
Eric Schlosser

With a Preface by Robert Redford and an Introduction by Eric Schlosser

# PENGUIN MODERN CLASSICS

**HERZOG**
SAUL BELLOW

With an Introduction by Malcolm Bradbury

'Spectacular ... surely Bellow's greatest novel' Malcolm Bradbury

This is the story of Moses Herzog, a great sufferer, joker, mourner and charmer. Although his life steadily disintegrates around him – he has failed as a writer and teacher, as a father, and has lost the affection of his wife to his best friend – Herzog sees himself as a survivor, both of his private disasters and those of the age. He writes unsent letters to friends and enemies, colleagues and famous people, revealing his wry perception of the world and the innermost secrets of his heart.

'A masterpiece ... Herzog's voice, for all its wildness and strangeness and foolishness, is the voice of a civilization, our civilization'
*The New York Times Book Review*

WINNER OF THE NOBEL PRIZE FOR LITERATURE

# PENGUIN MODERN CLASSICS

**LIGHT YEARS**
JAMES SALTER

'An American master of fiction' *Independent*

Negra and Viri are a couple whose enviable life is centred on civilized pleasures, their children, a variety of friends, and days lived to the utmost, be it skating on a frozen river or summers by the sea. It is a world built on matrimony, and its details – the one moment, one hour, one day – recapture everything.

But fine cracks are beginning to spread through the shimmering surface – flaws that will eventually mar the lovely picture beyond repair. Seductive, witty, tender and resonant, *Light Years* is a ravishing novel of lost lives and the elusiveness of happiness.

'Remarkable … a moving ode to beautiful lives frayed by time' *Esquire*

# PENGUIN MODERN CLASSICS

**LIBRA**
DON DELILLO

'An unparalleled trip into the heart of America' *Observer*

Exploring the tale behind the six seconds that broke the back of the American century, *Libra* combines fact, hypothesis and fiction to portray the events leading up to the assassination of John F. Kennedy on 22 November 1963.

Powerful and eerily convincing, it chronicles Lee Harvey Oswald's odyssey from troubled teenager to a man of precarious stability searching for a role in history. When 'history' presents itself in the form of three disaffected CIA operatives, the scales are irrevocably tipped as Oswald finds himself caught up in events far beyond his control.

'This you feel is America, and the bad news starts here' *Sunday Times*

# PENGUIN MODERN CLASSICS

**THE WOMAN IN THE DUNES**
KOBO ABE

With a new Introduction by David Mitchell

Translated by E. Dale Saunders

'A haunting Kafkaesque nightmare' *Time*

Niki Jumpei, an insect enthusiast, searches the scorching desert for beetles. As night falls he is forced to seek shelter in an eerie village, half-buried by huge sand dunes. He awakes to the terrifying realization that the villagers have imprisoned him in a steep-sided sand pit with no means of escape. Tricked into slavery and threatened with starvation if he does not work, Jumpei's only choice is to shovel the ever-encroaching sand – or face an agonizing death.

Amongst the greatest Japanese novels of the twentieth century, *The Woman in the Dunes* combines the essence of myth, suspense and the existential novel.

'Abe follows with meticulous precision his hero's constantly shifting physical, emotional and psychological states' *The New York Times*

# PENGUIN MODERN CLASSICS

**ANIMAL FARM**
GEORGE ORWELL

'It is the book for everyone and Everyman, its brightness undimmed after fifty years' Ruth Rendell, *Daily Telegraph*, Books of the Century

'It is the history of a revolution that went wrong – and of the excellent excuses that were forthcoming at every step for the perversion of the original doctrine,' wrote Orwell for the first edition of *Animal Farm* in 1945. Orwell wrote the novel at the end of 1943, but it almost remained unpublished. Its savage attack on Stalin, at that time Britain's ally, led to the book being refused by publisher after publisher. Orwell's simple, tragic fable, telling what happens after the animals drive out Mr Jones and attempt to run the farm themselves, has since become a world-famous classic.

With an Introduction by Malcolm Bradbury

THE AUTHORITATIVE TEXT

# PENGUIN MODERN CLASSICS

---

**THE DHARMA BUMS**
JACK KEROUAC

'A descriptive excitement unmatched since the days of Thomas Wolf' *The New York Times Book Review*

Following the explosive energy of *On the Road* comes *The Dharma Bums*, in which Kerouac charts the spiritual quest of a group of friends in search of Dharma, or Truth. Ray Smith and his friend Japhy, along with Morley the yodeller, head off into the high Sierras to seek the lesson of solitude and experience the Zen way of life. But in wildly bohemian San Francisco, with its poetry jam sessions, marathon drinking bouts and experiments in 'yabyum', they find the ascetic route distinctly hard to follow.

'A vivid evocation of a part of our time' *New York Post*

# PENGUIN MODERN CLASSICS

**DELIBERATE PROSE**
ALLEN GINSBERG

'The exemplary avant-garde figure of the post-war world' *Independent*

One of the key figures of twentieth-century American literary and cultural history, Allen Ginsberg was poet and prophet, revolutionary, political activist and a leading founder of the Beat Generation. Displaying a fantastic range of practical learning, this collection of his writings – essays, autobiographical fragments, letters, magazine articles – expresses his always unsettling and controversial thoughts on everything from the Vietnam war, freedom of speech, homosexuality and drug use, to the prose of Jack Kerouac and William S. Burroughs.

'A pioneer of openness and lifelong model of candour. Ginsberg stood for freedom of expression and for coming out of all the closets before others did' William S. Burroughs, *The New York Times*

Edited by Bill Morgan

# Penguin Modern Classics

---

**FIRST LOVE AND OTHER NOVELLAS**
SAMUEL BECKETT

THE END/ THE EXPELLED/ THE CALMATIVE/ FIRST LOVE

'He is the most courageous, remorseless writer going. He brings forth a body of beauty' Harold Pinter

Written in 1946, in what he later called 'a frenzy of writing', these four novellas are among the finest substantial works resulting from Beckett's decision to use French as his language of literary composition. Richly humorous, they offer a fascinating insight into preoccupations which remained constant throughout the work of a writer who transformed the art of the novel and contemporary theatre.

The aim of this new edition is to provide, as far as possible, the most accurate texts in English of the novellas.

Edited with an Introduction and Notes by Gerry Dukes

---

# Penguin Modern Classics

## GIOVANNI'S ROOM
JAMES BALDWIN

'Exquisite ... a feat of fire-breathing, imaginative daring' *Guardian*

David, a young American in 1950s Paris, is waiting for his fiancée to return from vacation in Spain. But when he meets Giovanni, a handsome Italian barman, the two men are drawn into an intense affair. After three months David's fiancée returns, and, denying his true nature, David rejects Giovanni for a 'safe' future as a married man. His decision eventually brings tragedy.

Full of passion, regret and longing, this story of a fated love triangle has become a landmark in gay writing, but its appeal is broader. James Baldwin caused outrage as a black author writing about white homosexuals, yet for him the issues of race, sexuality and personal freedom were eternally intertwined.

'Audacious ... remarkable ... elegant and courageous' Caryl Phillips

With a new Introduction by Caryl Phillips